THOSE "SUMMER OF '42" KIDS ARE BACK!

"I've enlisted," Benjie said.

"In what? The Boy Scouts?"

"The Marines."

"The Marines?"

"Yes."

"The United States Marines?" asked Oscy, completely nonplussed.

"Come on, Oscy," Benjie said.

"They took you? Your parents'll put the kibosh on that in five minutes. Your mother'll make Roosevelt sorry he was ever born."

Finally Hermie found his tongue. "Do you have your papers?"

Benjie took the papers out of his pocket and spread them on the table.

"I report in three weeks. Don't get chocolate on them, Hermie. I don't need chocolate-covered orders."

* * *

So the "terrible trio" was broken up. Hermie and Oscy obeyed their parents and went off to college, while Benjie—the uncoordinated, the least-likely-to-make-it, the unmatched—donned the uniform of his country and marched into the jaws of hell for Uncle Sam.

CLASS OF '44

Now A Major Motion Picture

Class of '44

by

Madeleine Shaner

Original screenplay by

Herman Raucher

Author of

Summer of '42

WARNER
PAPERBACK
LIBRARY

A Warner Communications Company

WARNER PAPERBACK LIBRARY EDITION

First Printing: April, 1973
Second Printing: May, 1973
Third Printing: May, 1973

Cover design by Bob Aulicino
Cover photo by Jarry Lang

**Warner Paperback Library is a division of Warner Books, Inc.,
315 Park Avenue South, New York, N.Y. 10010.**

Ⓦ A Warner Communications Company

Class of '44

1

Hermie looked around the auditorium which was conservatively aglow now with navy blue caps and gowns, all bobbing and swaying in a massive wave of excitement, relief, tension and fake boredom. Hermie felt that he'd waited so long for this moment that it was almost anti-climactic. He'd gone through it in his head a million times. He'd tripped on the steps up to the rostrum, he'd dropped his diploma, he'd fallen into the lap of the Principal's wife, as she sat, spread-legged, on the stage, he'd arrived late when all the graduation exercises were over. He'd even dreamed that he couldn't find the school and was wandering the streets of Brooklyn, like a nincompoop in a scarlet cap and gown, trying to find his way in a completely strange city. Just when he'd caught sight of school, good old Erasmus Hall, it'd disappeared into a playful nimbus, faded away like a desert mirage. Many's the time he'd wished it would disappear. But not now.

For almost the first time in his life he felt as if he really belonged to something, had a place somewhere. He was a part, a very necessary part, of the Graduating Class of 1944. Hermie Green, Class of '44. He tried it on for sound. Class of '44. Sounded kind of classy. H.G. '44. It would look good on his job application when he became Senior Editor of the New York Times, or maybe on the book cover of his best-selling novel about his war experiences.

There'd been some question about whether to hold graduation exercises at all because, as everyone wanted to inform you 'there's a war on, you know'. Oscy thought they should have just one enormous brawl instead, since they were all about to march into the jaws of Hell, or College, whichever came first. Benjie, who used words like 'behoove', said it behooved them to have graduation exercises because they're for the parents anyway. Gave them something to look forward to, and back on, now that they were getting on in years. Anyway, it was finally decided, by the Student Union and the Faculty, that the festivities would be kept to a minimum, there'd be no senior prom, and the band, which'd lost some of its more pertinent members to the Army, would be replaced by Miss Doyle at the piano.

Hermie was glad they'd decided to keep something. It was good for the parents and besides, being part of the pomp and circumstance gave you kind of a tingly feeling, like just before you dived into a swimming pool, or the second before the gun went off at a track meet. He supposed if you wanted to be grand about it you could go into all that Valedictorian stuff about standing on the threshold of life, looking down the corridors of the future, with the firm base of your high school years behind you . . . all that crap. He'd been standing on the threshold for so long he'd worn out the door-sill. He looked at himself in the shiny barrette of the girl in front of him. His face was red and slightly sweaty. He didn't look quite the suave, graduating man that he'd programmed for himself.

In fact, if he were being honest, he didn't feel any older today than he had yesterday, and certainly no more like Cary Grant than he had then. And he still felt fourteen. He bent over and surreptitiously wiped his upper lip on the corner of the rented gown. He looked around the room. Just across the aisle was an ostentatiously empty chair that had to be Oscy's. If he could manage it, Oscy would be late to his own funeral. Sure enough, there he was, cap askew, gown wrinkled as though the cat had napped in it, elbowing his way through the file of students that was serenely filling up the front rows of the auditorium. Oscy flopped down with a sigh and blew a blond tousle up against the crazily-angled cap. He looked over and caught Hermie's eye. From beneath the eye-level of any watching teachers he directed a double V-sign at Hermie. He did it with such force and vitality that it came across as more obscene than patriotic. Hermie grinned and turned away, looking for Benjie.

True to form, Benjie was standing in a side aisle, directing students to seats that had already been assigned. No one was paying the slightest attention to him but he had to have a function, to feel needed. His gown looked as if his mother had starched it that morning. It stood out from his skinny body in celestial wings. He could've taken off on a wing and a prayer at any moment. He attended to business very seriously, timing each group of ten students as they took their places. As the last of the boys and girls entered, Benjie looked around for his place. It was occupied. He leaned over and glowered at the boy who was sitting there. The boy shrugged, totally unmoved by Benjie's wrath, and turned away, not even interrupting his conversation with a friend in the next seat. Benjie looked around then sighing pettishly, stumbled over the outstretched feet of a dozen boys to take his place next to Mr. Eckert, the dourest and least friendly teacher on the faculty.

In among the caps and gowns were a few uniforms,

some Army, a couple of Navy and a few Marines. Boys who had already enlisted had been permitted to come back to get their diplomas. They stood out, like exotic birds, out of uniform in their uniforms.

The parents were already seated, rustling programs, women buzzing in new hats, fathers uncomfortable as always in folding school chairs. Here and there a uniform shone out like a badge of belonging in the motley parent sea.

Hermie looked for his mother and father. He quickly spotted his mother in last year's grey suit, with its squared-off shoulders and this year's heavy-seined pink hairnet gathered up into fake anemones in back of her upswept hairdo. She had her arm tightly through his father's, wrinkling the sleeve of his 'good' suit. They both looked on edge, as if they were afraid he might not make it. He tried not to catch his mother's eye. She might come over and ask him if he had to go to the bathroom first.

Everyone finally squeezed into the hall, soaking up its normal sepulchral echo into the warmth of their joint body. Somewhere up front, Miss Doyle, supremely self-important in her conspicuous role, was rippling off her favorite arpeggio, the only one she knew, and the choir stumbled into 'Land of Hope and Glory' as the last graduates filed in.

The Principal, high on his dais, signalled for everyone to stand and face the flag. His son, a Lieutenant in the Air-Force, led the Pledge of Allegiance. Then, shuffling and rustling, the entire audience wheezed into the National Anthem as Miss Doyle quickly changed the music in front of her. Difficult as it was to sing, and with half the people not knowing the words as usual, it still made Hermie shiver and goose-pimple under his gown. He sang with the others, suddenly serious and listening to the words for the first time. Off to the left Hermie could hear Oscy, louder than everybody else, competing with the piano for first place. If Oscy couldn't win, he wasn't playing. Benjie, off on his own keyboard, somewhere in the key of J, was testing the mettle of those at either side of him. The boy next to him raised his eyes heavenward as Benjie hit a particularly harmonious K flat.

The anthem over, the Principal gestured, papally, to the audience to be seated. And they were seated. And it was good. Hermie concentrated on the copy of the Dürer portrait of Erasmus over the Principal's head. The old theologian's eyes twinkled out frostily from under the funny hat. Hermie distinctly saw the head nod its approval of the five-hundred graduates, with an extra-special nod for Hermie. "Thanks," Hermie whispered, "I needed that."

Hermie missed the first five minutes of Dr. Brenzinger's speech. It had the ring of familiarity and he didn't expect to be tested on it, so he wasn't too concerned. Anyway, he remembered his sister's graduation, and Oscy said if you'd heard one, you'd heard 'em all.

The Principal droned on. "As we come to your final days at dear old Erasmus High we, your Principal and Faculty, note with sadness how many of the class of '44 have already joined the forces of freedom and democracy. I have the unpleasant task of informing you at this time that we have also had our first loss from the Class of '43. Victor Yates, who was our Class Valedictorian this time last year, was reported killed in action yesterday, somewhere over Germany."

There was a dreadful, awed silence in the hall. Hermie had known Victor only by sight. Suddenly the war was very real. Hermie caught Oscy's eye again. This time he saw the same goddamned question he'd been seeing there for weeks. Hermie rubbed his chin and wished for more stubble. If he had more beard, maybe he'd know more. Whiskers and wisdom were supposed to have something to do with each other. He shook his head at Oscy, not saying no, just dismissing his question, and turned his attention back to Erasmus.

"Yes," the Principal went on, directing his answer to Hermie. "Some of you will go on to college, and some into the business world . . . but others of you will don uniforms of your country and join the battle. . . ." Those already in uniform self-consciously changed cheeks as the other students turned to look at them. "Yours, we also note, is the last class to have entered Erasmus Hall when our country was still at peace."

The applause drowned out the beginning of the Grade Advisor's speech. Hermie felt the applause was not just for the Principal's speech, but for the boy who had given his life for his country, for his parents who must be suffering now, for the boys in uniform in the Hall, and for all the people in the world who had felt and were feeling war.

The Grade Advisor was a nervous, stringy woman, with a high, unresonant voice. She had jumped into the breach before it was open. Her face was red and she looked ill at ease. Some of the more heartless graduates, with Oscy in the lead, renewed their applause for the Principal, so that he had to lift his heavenly arms for silence while the Grade Advisor tracked back to her opening. Benjie looked around disapprovingly at his fellow students and sat up straighter to compensate for their insensitivity. The uncomfortable woman began. "As you go forth, citizens of our Old Grey School, remember that we who stay on will be judged by you. Be worthy of our school's traditions; face today's problems with today's courage. . . ."

Under his breath, Oscy hissed, "And yesterday's underwear," causing the girl in front of him to collapse in giggles, which had been his intention.

"And do not forget that always . . ." the stringy one went on, trying to control the tear that had etched its way down to the tip of her aristocratic nose, "Do not forget . . ." Unfortunately she had left her glasses at home, out of a misplaced pride, and was having trouble reading her notes. She found her place, and sniff! There she finally had that drip! "Do not forget that always, standing by, there is ONE who will strengthen and comfort you . . . whether at home, at college, or in the midst of battle. . . . HE is there with you."

Oscy swallowed back a smart-ass remark as Hermie, anticipating one, glared at him from across the aisle.

As the graduates were called up for their diplomas, Hermie heard his name called, and managed, without tripping or falling into the Principal's wife's lap, to make it down the aisle and up onto the stage. Diploma clutched in his damp palm, he managed a wink at Erasmus before he descended into the auditorium. Erasmus winked back.

The important part of the ceremony over, only one set of parents remained tensely attentive as the Valedictorian, a pretty, blonde-haired girl with bouncy breasts and bobby sox, made a terribly symbolic speech about robins flying against windows, that nobody quite understood.

Again the Papal wave and the audience rose for the Alma Mater, lustily sung by the owners of three hundred pairs of cramped limbs and crumpled seats.

> "Old Grey School that cast a spell,
> On us all your blessings fell;
> Men and women born of thee . . .
> Breathe the air that makes them free.
> Alma Mater . . .
> Blessed one . . .
> Farewell."

Total confusion as students and audience, released from the confines of total subjection, immediately began milling around, hugging, kissing, back-slapping, hand-shaking, raising a roar that would've drowned out an air-raid alert. The Faculty, temporarily deserted, huddled together for mutual solace near the piano.

"Play a march!" the Principal hissed at Miss Doyle, "We're way over the room capacity. Let's get 'em moving."

Miss Doyle swung gallantly into "Battle Hymn of the

Republic" as the crowd, with Pavlovian reflexes, began to move out into the corridor.

Mothers, antennae flying, made perfect three-point landings on sons and daughters. Hermie's mother, always a front-runner in the Mother Stakes, descended on him like the Assyrians coming down. Hermie tried to dodge, but only with half a heart, since he knew he was on the losing side in this battle. "Hermie, I was trying to catch your eye before. You always get so nervous. I wanted to make sure you went to the bathroom." Hermie smiled at his own intuition and let himself be hugged amply, all the time looking around to make sure no one noticed. No one noticed. Everyone else was too busy looking around to make sure no one noticed *they* were being hugged. Aunt Mae and Aunt Tess moved in for the kill but they weren't so familiar with Hermie's battle strategy, and he was into Phase Two by the time they'd called their signals. Phase Two involved shaking hands with Dad, who mumbled something about being proud of him and pressed a twenty-dollar bill into Hermie's hand. His sister, not expecting it, met Hermie in a head-on as he leaned in to give her a peck on the cheek.

Hermie made his escape, colliding with every other boy in the school who'd had the same idea. The families were left to congratulate each other. Ernie Price, the custodian, began to sweep up around the feet of the victorious clans, making his non-verbal statement in the most subtle way he knew. Hermie was half-way across the schoolyard before his father caught up with him.

"Hi, Dad."

"Hi, son." His father was always uncomfortable in direct confrontation. "Look, want to have a bite somewhere?"

"You and me?"

"Yeah, your mother wants to go home and start baking. Where would you like to go?"

Hermie shrugged. Carsten's was the only place he

knew intimately and it was hardly right for a father-and-son talk.

"Dubrow's all right?"

Hermie shrugged again. That was the way the conversation mostly went when he was with his father. Question? Shrug. Question? Shrug. Question? Shrug. It came in the manual.

Hermie led the way through knots of capped-and-gowned students until they reached the street. He stayed half a pace in front of his father, just in case anyone should misunderstand and think he was going to have lunch with the old man. They passed a number of other boys whose steps were being dogged by older men who bore a distinct family resemblance.

2

Hermie had been in Dubrow's before. It was the only place his family could ever think of when they wanted to celebrate, and it was ideal because everybody could have what they wanted and it didn't cost too much.

It was a bit late for lunch in Brooklyn, so the lines at the cafeteria counter weren't too long. The people dining there seemed to be mainly businessmen, and an occasional, tired woman shopper who had to get off her feet for ten minutes. There were also a number of those unusual twosomes that'd drifted in Hermie and his father's wake from the High School.

Hermie followed his father through the line. His father had the pot roast, with mashed potatoes and some green beans. Hermie had fried chicken and spaghetti, a combination that raised the eyebrows of the cashier a bit higher than the ones she'd so carefully pencilled on that morning. Hermie had a Pepsi and his father had coffee.

The found a table near the window. Neither of them

spoke as they unloaded their trays and unwrapped the cutlery from its napkin.

Hermie looked around. "It's ages since I was here. Food's okay, though."

His father accepted Hermie's approval.

He leaned in and cleared his throat. "Herm . . . Hermie, I wanted to talk to you alone, man to man . . . there hasn't been time."

"I know." Hermie knew what this was all about but he didn't feel like helping.

"I think I know how you feel. I was in World War One."

"I know."

"But you've got a deferment. You can go to college and get your degree."

"Without feeling guilty," Hermie finished for him.

His father flushed. "Look, the war's going to be over soon anyway."

"I feel like a shit just staying home and going to school with all the 4-Fs." He didn't normally use words like 'shit' around his father, but nothing was said, so he supposed it was all right when it was just men.

"I told you . . . I know how you feel. But you're our only son. Al will be going. Ruth and he have only been married a couple of months . . ."

"Al's nothing to do with me."

"He's your sister's husband."

"But he felt *he* had to go and he's married, for Chrissakes. I'm not even married!"

"You're only eighteen. Get in a year of college . . . just one year, then we'll talk again, okay?"

"I've been accepted at Connecticut but I don't have to go. I could still enlist.

"It's really up to you of course but I beg you to think of your mother."

It wasn't up to him. Putting it like that made it very clear to Hermie, it wasn't up to him. It was up to his mother and his father and his sister, and his sister's husband, and his School Principal and the Old Maid Grade Advisor and the goddamned Valedictorian and maybe the Queen of England for all he knew. "Excuse me, Queen, can I . . . may I serve in the United States Army?" "Oh, no indeed, laddie, the University of Connecticut and your mother need you!" "Why, thank you, Queen. It will be my lordly pleasure."

He returned to his father. "Some of the guys've already gone."

"It's up to you." His father wiped his mustache before embarking on his pot roast, which seemed to Hermie like wiping your feet before you went out into the street.

Hermie out-stared the chicken and spaghetti in front of him. On the under-side of a chicken leg he found a flashing neon sign that lit up each time he chewed. "We can't all fight, but we can all help!" the sign announced. He didn't believe it and turned the leg over. Sure enough the sign moved to the under-side again. This time it read: "Turn in waste fats *regularly*!" "They should've turned this in," he mumbled to himself.

"What did you say?" asked his father.

"I said I think this spaghetti sauce is made with Spam," Hermie said.

"It probably is," his father sighed. "After all, you know, there's a war on!"

"You ain't just clickin' your teeth," Hermie reassured him, grimly chewing on chicken bones.

3

His mother seemed to have invited thousands of people to the Graduation party. Hermie knew most of them, although there were a couple of relatives he wished they'd kept the news from. He'd been jostled by everyone in the whole of New York State who had even a drop of the Green blood, which included a couple of distant cousins he'd never met before and hoped he'd never meet again. All Hermie's friends were there, except Benjie, who'd been, most likely, waylaid by Ocean Parkway. There were people in every room of the second floor of the two-family house—on the stairs, in the bedroom, in the kitchen, coming out of the walls. Hermie even detected a couple under the carpet, but he stomped them out before they could arise and kiss him.

His mother had been hoarding sugar and spice since Hermie was in kindergarten, so there were cakes and cookies enough for the whole of the U.S. Armed Forces, sandwiches, salads, pretzels, Pepsis, Dr. Browns, candy.

There were girls too, just the 'nice' ones. What his mother didn't know about the others wouldn't hurt her. One of them, Margie Lewis, tried trailing Hermie through the melee, but was constantly being sidetracked by well-wishing friends who wanted to give her farewell hugs in corners. From time to time Hermie looked back to see if she was still with him, and once he rescued her from Old King Kong himself, Oscy. But he wasn't very interested in Margie Lewis, so he finally let her fade in his wake, while he went in search of happiness, or at least solitude, outside on the stairs.

The stairwell was lined with others of the same persuasion, drinking cokes and coffee, and a few, away from their own M.P.s, that is Mother Patrols, patriotically smoking "Lucky Strikes," the cigarette that had joined the War Effort.

Oscy slapped Hermie on the back. Hermie tried to remember where he knew him from. "Was it Monte Carlo in '28? . . . or Mardi Gras in New Orleans in '36?. . . . Ah, now I remember, Erasmus Hall, Class of '44! My God, how you've changed, old man!"

"Hey, Hermie," Oscy said, ignoring the whole elaborate performance. "Nice party! Where's Benjie?"

"I don't know. And my mother made orange layer cake, special for him." Hermie squeezed on to a stair, between Paulie Marcus and a girl Paulie was trying to get to know better, much better. Paulie glared at him with the hatred that only an eighteen-year old can feel when he's cut in on.

"I don't suppose it matters, but this place is a fire trap," Hermie said, coughing. "Who's smoking a cigar?"

"I am," a girl called from below.

Everybody laughed. Oscy sat down on the step in back of Hermie. "My mother's having my diploma bronzed. Can that be done?" He was playing to the gallery, as usual.

"Your mother's the one who can do it," Hermie said.

A pretty girl passed by, climbing the stairs on the way up to the apartment. Her leg brushed Oscy's cheek. He swooned in ecstasy and lay, prostrate, on the stair.

"Anybody seen Lorraine?" she asked.

From his excellent viewing position, Oscy tried to look up her skirt. "Who's she with?"

The girl pulled her skirt tight around her legs. Oscy wasn't an unknown quantity in her circle. "Jerry Miller, I think."

"Try the bedroom." Oscy winked elaborately and nudged Hermie with his elbow. "That Lorraine, heh, Hermie? Ever get her into your bedroom?"

Hermie looked around to see who was listening, then frowned at Oscy. "Shut up, Oscy."

"Who're you with?"

"Margie Lewis."

"You're kidding. You're out of your groove!"

"She's my cousin. The family's been keeping her a secret." Hermie apologized.

"I'd have her bronzed and be done with it," Oscy said, disgusted.

Paulie Marcus leaned over and asked, "Hey, Hermie . . . when you going in?"

"Never," replied Hermie.

"Aren't you 1-A?"

"I'm going to college. Educational Deferment First Class." He stood and saluted.

Paulie looked down his nose, what there was of it. "Oh . . . that's very nice. I mean . . . that's okay."

"Cut it, Paulie," said Oscy. "If you had the marks Hermie had, you'd be going to college too."

"There's a war on, remember?" Paulie sneered.

"Yeah, I've heard the rumor," Oscy said sweetly.

"If you enlist you can pick your own branch. I'm going into the Navy," Paulie said, loud enough for the girl at the other side of Hermie to hear.

"As what?" Oscy asked. "A torpedo?"

Paulie tried smiling to see how it felt. It felt safe. "Good old Oscy," he said, pounding Oscy's back a bit harder than he'd intended.

"You'll have scurvy in a week," Oscy shouted after Paulie. He ran his hand through his messy hair and sighed. "Damn it, Hermie. What the hell are we doing going to college?"

Hermie had been planning his answer ever since lunch with his father. He'd decided to show no emotion, take no sides, just somehow live through the questions and maybe the rest of his life, without letting anything touch him. He gave his newly-minted, stock answer now. "We're going to complete our education."

"My education is complete. I know when Columbus discovered America and I been laid six times. What else *is* there?" Oscy looked around for applause.

"How about literature? Poetry?" Hermie said.

"Damn it, Hermie . . . I feel like a goddamned slacker! Christ, we're officer material, you and me. In 90 days we could be Lieutenants."

Calm, Hermie, stay calm. "In 90 days we'll be Freshmen."

"Well, I'll tell you . . . I'm not staying in college. I mean . . . I'll give it a couple weeks because I promised my father. After that, unless there's some special attraction on campus, like a Jap landing party, I'm enlisting."

"Sure."

"I mean it."

"I know."

Oscar was getting very red in the face. He looked ready to burst. He was regretting that the 'Fuck-you-Hermie' 'Fuck-you-Oscy' days were over. He looked around angrily. "Phyliss Ettinger? Where are you? Advance and be recognized!"

"Down here."

"We're leaving."

"Okay."

Oscy relented and smiled down at Hermie. "I'm gonna grab her boobs right in her father's car." He dangled the keys. "Little did he know, eh?" He started down the stairs. "Meet you at Carstens about midnight?"

"Okay."

"Hubba-hubba." Oscy tromped down the stairs, not overtly making any efforts to avoid outstretched hands and feet. "Careless hands cost lives," he whispered into the ear of one of the boys he'd "accidentally" stomped. "Gangway, folks. And don't panic, but . . . there's a small fire upstairs. A Nazi pyromaniac got hold of all our diplomas and now we have to do the whole thing over. . . ." He departed in the blaze of his public personality, leaving everyone around slightly singed and losing light.

Hermie got up and went back inside, hoping the crowds'd maybe thinned a little. But the apartment was still jam-packed with the same milling relatives, all waiting for the magic moment when they could pinch his cheek or pat his little head. Hermie had made a vow years before that when he was an aged relative, he'd never, never pinch cheeks. Noone could know just how much it hurt, if he'd never had his cheek pinched. Maybe he'd even make a law when he became Ambassador to Okinawa that no person should ever pinch another person's cheek, on penalty of immediate emasculation. He had a few other good laws in mind. Most of them dealt with relatives and the unbelievable liberties they took. Some of them dealt with mothers, but they would have to be passed in secret session, because mothers had very long ears.

Hermie steered through the massed ranks of the First Green Infantry Division. To avoid conversation he had stuffed his mouth full of orange layer cake, and when anyone asked him anything, he pointed to his full mouth as if to say, "I can't talk, my tongue has been cut out."

His mother was madly re-filling plates to stave off imminent starvation of the populace. One of the pledges she'd given when she's been elected to Mother was that in *her* house nobody would ever go hungry. So far she'd kept her election-eve pledge. Neither snow, nor rain, nor heat, nor gloom of night stayed her from her appointed rounds, a cookie here, a sandwich, a piece of cake, a pear, a glass of punch there. At the risk of upsetting her, Hermie ducked into a bedroom. It was full of boys, on the bed, on the floor, on the bureau, one boy precariously perched on the window sill.

"I report in two weeks," one of the boys was saying. "Eight weeks basic, and then to the Pacific . . . I *think*. I mean I put in for the Seabees."

"Did you see that poem the Seabees wrote? It was in a magazine. Something about entering Tokyo on the roads the Seabees built. Something like that."

"I saw where a guy called Andrew Tokio had to change his name . . ."

"My problem's my eyes. They keep turning me down. Jesus . . . how small are the Japs?"

"That's okay. There's things you can do as a civilian. . ."

"Like what?"

"Buy only what you need. Pay no more than ceiling prices," some wag called out from the bed. He was quoting slogans from newspaper ads.

"Ha-ha! You can be a riveter or a welder. Work in a defense plant."

Somebody noticed Hermie who was standing with his back against the door, his mouth and his whole being feeling as if it were stuffed with orange layer cake.

"What about you, Hermie? When you going in?"

Hermie was fed up with the question. He was fed up with the party. "I'm too old. Also, I have a wooden leg, and a heart murmur, and a punctured eardrum, and one of you son-of-a-bitches stepped in dog-shit. . . ." He escaped, letting the door bang behind him.

If he walked down the street a couple of miles, maybe he'd meet someone who wouldn't know him well enough to ask him any more questions. He didn't feel right about walking out of his own graduation party, but it'd been just too long a day; there'd been too much talk; too many questions; too much had happened. He felt as if he were suffocating. Anyway, his mother didn't know he'd gone, an absolute first in Hermie's entire life. He walked down to the Park, noticing all the things he didn't want to notice; the gold star in Mrs. Schwartz' window, for Elliott, killed at El Alamein; the brave little Victory Garden that Crazy Alf, the paper boy, was cultivating on the corner of a vacant lot; the sign posted in the butcher's window SAVE WASTE FATS FOR EXPLOSIVES; the two kids wheeling a beat-up baby buggy piled high with tin cans and old newspapers; the A sticker in the corner of the rear window of a Chevy that had seen better days; the BUY WAR BONDS poster plastered over the subway entrance sign. He veered to avoid a guy on crutches in army uniform, with one pants leg fastened up to his waist with a baby's diaper pin.

Everything had gotten so complicated. He wished he were back in an easier time when all you had to decide was which college to go to, or what your major should be, or whether to try bare titty with Elsie Loomis at the show on Saturday night.

He reached the park and sat down dejectedly on a bench, his chin in his hand, the Thinker, thinking of nothing, looking at nothing. A young girl was handing out leaflets. He took one automatically, not reading it, but crumpling it into a ball as he sat there. On his way home he absent-mindedly opened up the leaflet, flattening it to see the lowering brow of a fierce Uncle Sam staring out at him, saying: I WANT *YOU* FOR THE U.S. ARMY. ENLIST NOW.

4

Hermie wandered into Carsten's about midnight and looked around for Oscy. Every booth was jammed, mostly with boys, it being past bedtime for all self-respecting girls' mothers. Mother (muth'er), n. someone who makes you wear a sweater when she feels cold. It worked the same for bedtimes, too, especially for girls, though Hermie had often wondered what it was you could do that would be so terrible after midnight that you couldn't do just as well before. The juke-box was pouring out "Swingin' on a Star" with Bing Crosby giving his all to the question of who'd rather be a mule. The joint was especially crowded tonight, probably because of graduation. A couple of boys were doing a weird Lindy in time with some inner rhythm that had nothing to do with Bing's crooning. Hermie watched for a minute, then quickly dived into a booth as a young couple moved out. As the girl slid out of the booth she said to the boy, "I don't dare. My mother'd have a fit."

"I'm not asking your mother to do it," the boy answered.

Wonder what that was all about, thought Hermie, as if I couldn't guess. He sat there unnoticed for a while, bits of conversations hitting him like enemy flak from all sides.

"I mean, I'm breaking my nails on her idiot brassiere and just when I'm ready to throw in the towel . . . whammo . . . one silent move from her and the whole thing miraculously comes free."

"My major will be marketing but I'll be minoring in advertising and journalism."

"I hear they have a great *black* marketing course at CCNY."

"You can't dance when you're like that."

"No way. Not without her knowing you're excited. Christ, I'm holding her real close but my ass is in the Goddamned punchbowl."

"So I tell her I'm shipping out in a week and she goes all limp with patriotism, and her eyes go glassy . . ."

"Shipping out? You're going to *NYU*."

"You don't volunteer that information, stupid."

"Oh."

"So, her eyes go glassy and . . ."

Hermie had ordered a banana split. On top of all the orange layer cake he'd put away earlier, it wasn't too comfortable a fit, but he wasn't paying too much attention to what he was eating. He wasn't crazy about being alone in places where there were hundreds of people. He didn't get along well with crowds and wished Oscy would hurry up. Just then someone leaned over Hermie's shoulder and in a very serious voice said, "I gotta tell you, Hermie, I hate that 'Swingin' on a Star."

Hermie jumped slightly, then recovered. "It's not my nickel."

Oscy stood up on the seat of the booth and shouted at the top of his lungs to anyone who was listening, "Which one of you morons played that song? Twenty lashes and bread and water for a week." A couple of boys booed, but no one volunteered to accept Oscy's wrath. He climbed down and went over to the jukebox, put in a nickel and came back to the table. "I'm in the mood for romance."

"How'd you make out?"

"Hit the horn three times and the jackpot once. Where the hell's Benjie?"

"I don't know. Probably tripped over a puddle."

"Poor kid. Still doesn't know which end is up."

"Swingin' on a Star" finally groaned to an end and was followed by "Long Ago and Far Away." Oscar reacted with a fake swoon, all across the table, almost into Hermie's ice cream. "Ah, there it is. Our Song . . . me and Phyliss." He swayed to the music, like a lovesick violinist. "A love affair has to have a song to mark it, Hermie. That's one of the first rules."

"No fooling."

"Yeah, to make it memorable." He closed his eyes again and mooned to his memories. "From now on, whenever I hear that song, I'll think of Phyliss Ettinger."

"That's a fast way to ruin a good song," Hermie said.

"You have a dry sense of humor, Hermie. Not funny . . . but dry." Oscy leaned over and poured the remainder of Herm's water glass over his friend's head.

Fortunately the glass was almost empty. Hermie looked up and saw Benjie winding his way to their table, tripping regularly over his own feet. "Here he comes," said Hermie.

Benjie didn't look like much. Whatever he put together in the way of clothes never seemed to work. You wanted to go check out his wardrobe and rearrange it so that the orange shirt somehow could make its escape from the green striped jeans that must have been his sister's, before she developed taste. Tonight he was wearing rolled-up blue jeans, which was all right, but black dress socks didn't make it, and his jacket had more affinity with paternity than fraternity, and his father was bigger than

he was. He looked around the room, not quite seeing
them through his moontinted spectacles, but veering in
their general direction. Oscy stuck his foot out into the
aisle, and obligingly Benjie fell over it, exactly according
to the script. He tripped into the booth, a typical entrance.
Benjie had a funny look on his face. Hermie noticed it
right off and then wondered why Benjie hadn't shown up
at the graduation party.

The waitress had followed Benjie to the booth. She
planted herself a hundred-and-fifty pounds square in front
of Oscy and sniffed, indicating they'd better not try to get
away without ordering something. She'd served kids long
enough to know that one soda and three straws was the
general rule if they could get away with it.

Benjie pointed to Hermie's banana split. "I'll have what
he's having." Then, an afterthought, "What are you having, Hermie?"

"Heartburn."

The waitress stolidly dictated to herself as she wrote,
"Banana split, vanilla cream, fudge sauce. You?" she
asked Oscy.

"Same."

She went through the whole procedure again, in the
same detail, then thundered off, her heavy tread synco-
pating the rhythm of the jukebox.

"Sorry I missed your party, Hermie."

"Forget it."

Oscy delighted in making people feel guilty. "His
mother made orange layer cake . . . especially for you.
Five of 'em."

Benjie managed to look a little shaken. "That's very
thoughtful of her. Please give your mother my thanks."

"Give them to her yourself. There's still two left," said
Hermie.

Benjie looked about to burst with his secret. "I may
not be able to thank her personally. THIS IS IT!" He said
the last with the smile Van Johnson had perfected for

dumping his bombload over Mannheim. On Benjie, however, it came out more like Harpo Marx laying an egg. He paused for another dramatic moment, while Oscy and Hermie just stared at him. Bomb doors open, here we go boys, this one for der Führer . . . Bombs away! "I'VE ENLISTED."

There was a dead silence while the poor people of Mannheim collected their scattered households and repaired to the nearest Autobahn to begin their refugee trek to the next town to be bombed.

At last Oscy found his tongue. "In what? The Boy Scouts?"

"The Marines."

"The Marines?!"

"Yes."

"The United States Marines?" asked Oscy, completely non-plussed.

"Come on, Oscy," Benjie said.

"They took you?"

"Jesus, Oscy . . ."

Oscy stood up and addressed the multitude. "War's over, folks. We lose."

Benjie got angry. "Goddam, Oscy, quit p-putting me down, you've been doing it for years. Stop already!!"

Oscy sat down again, not yet ready to turn in his attitude but a bit chastened by Benjie's attack. "What the hell you doing enlisting in the Marines, Benjie?"

"I want to fight for my country . . . is that so goddamned strange?"

"Your parents'll put the kibosh on it in five minutes. Your mother'll make Roosevelt sorry he was ever born." Oscy scoffed, a full-blown tyrant again. He was, after all, the leader, the one who initiated everything. To have Benjie usurp his position like that . . . Benjie, the least-likely-to-make-it member of the old Terrible Trio. Benjie, the un-matched. Benjie, the uncoordinated. Benjie, the

fearful. Benjie the sleep-walker. Benjie?!! He couldn't
accept it.

Benjie had somehow grown a couple of inches since
he'd dropped his bombs. "I'm of age. When I sign my
name . . . it sticks. I'm going. I'm in. It's official."

Hermie finally unfroze his tongue. "Do you have your
papers?"

Benjie took them out of his jacket pocket. The bulk of
them was probably one of the reasons the jacket had
looked so shapeless, though only one of the reasons,
because even with the papers removed it still retained all
of Benjie's father's bulges. He spread the papers carefully
out on the table in front of them. "I report in three weeks.
Don't get chocolate on them, Hermie. I don't need chocolate-covered orders." It was a joke. Trouble with Benjie's
jokes, they were never funny. Like his clothes, they somehow didn't make it.

"When the hell did you enlist?" asked Oscy. "During
the Alma Mater?"

"A couple of weeks ago. I went into Times Square.
They have a Recruitment Booth. They were very nice
about it." Benjie's ice cream had been dumped in front
of him. He dug in like a Seabee digging a latrine.

"Bet your boots they were nice about it," Oscy said.
"Another lamb to the slaughter. Some war. If you ask me
it's a phony war."

Hermie looked at Oscy in amazement. "Oscy, you don't
believe that! You want to go yourself."

"Yeah, well I changed my mind. Who wants to go
fight Roosevelt's war?" Oscy dug into his banana split,
and with the first dig changed his mind again. He leaned
over to Benjie. "Listen . . . can I borrow these papers?
If I show my father that you went in . . . Shit, if the
Marines took *you* . . . I mean, you can't go in by yourself,
Benjie. You can't go *anywhere* by yourself."

Benjie decided not to nurse hurt feelings. He could rise
above anything Oscy had to throw at him. "Those days

are over, Oscy. Over and gone." There was a certain dramatic finality to his words.

"They'll cut off your hair. Your beautiful, curly hair. Your mother'll take the gas-pipe."

Benjie ignored him. He was eating and talking at the same time, the chocolate sauce dribbling down his chin and back into the dish, occasionally finding a target on his shirt-front, which had been none-too-clean to begin with. "I wanted an outfit with some tradition, some honor. I know it's corny but . . . it's done. And," he paused for effect, also to lick his chin, "I'm looking forward to it. I hope I get into battle; I don't care where. Guadalcanal, the Philippines . . . it doesn't matter . . . Wherever I'm sent, I'll go. It'll be fine." He pounded his fist on the table, sending whipped cream flying in all directions. Oscy, whose normal reaction to anything that didn't please him was to laugh it out of existence, was about to say "They'll laugh themselves to death!" Then he thought better of it, for the first time in his life, and didn't say a word.

Benjie was well into his stride now, cheered on by his own daring, both at joining up and at doing it without consulting Oscy. "Damn it, when they attacked our country . . . well . . . I'm going to get into it. And I'm going to be . . . very proud." He stood and waved his spoon, surprising the hell out of the waitress who had just dropped by with the check.

Oscy raised his water glass in a toast and began to sing, "From the Halls of Montezuma,
   To the shores of Tripoli;
   We will eat our orange layer cake
   On the land and on the sea."

His singing mingled incongruously with "Swingin' on a Star," which someone had punched on again, and pretty soon was drowned out by the chatter and friendly kidding of a bunch of teenaged kids. There wasn't much of a war going on in Carsten's.

Hermie had pretty well come to terms with his own ambivalence, if that wasn't a contradiction in terms. He respected his folks' wishes. They'd always been all right with him. On the other hand, there was Benjie, old two-left-shoe Benjie, going into the Marines. On the other hand, Hermie wasn't sure he really wanted to go into the Army, even if he did make protestations from time to time. He wasn't by nature a joiner, nor was he big at making statements. On the other hand, so many of the boys were gone and a couple even dead, it made you feel guilty. Then he asked himself if he were a coward. He didn't think so. He'd knocked out Johnny Stella hadn't he? 'Course that was because Oscy'd told him to. He needed to be told what to do. People like him were supposed to make the best soldiers. It was always the rebel who didn't make out in army pictures. "We're paying you to obey orders, soldier, not to think." "Yes, sir!" But that guy was always the hero in the end. He was the one who dragged ten of his wounded buddies back to base, or limped home in his big DeHaviland bomber with one broken wing and the tail on fire. Hermie wasn't a hero. He knew that. On the other hand, he really wanted to go to college. He'd liked what he'd seen at Connecticut when he'd gone there for his interview. And somebody had to keep the home fires burning. On the other hand . . . Hermie decided he'd probably gone through a dozen and a half hands already, so he stopped thinking about it.

He was lying on his bed and could hear The Duke jazzing it up on the Bob Hope Show in the other room. He picked up a magazine and began to read.

He fell asleep with a picture stencilled on his eyelids, of Benjie, broken and twisted, in a too-big Marine uniform, lying on a rock in the Pacific Ocean, calling out, "I didn't mean it, Oscy. It was just a joke!"

5

There was a long summer ahead. School was over. It was about a hundred and one years before the new semester at Conn. Hermie and Oscy had taken jobs in the shipping room of a wholesale drug warehouse. It wasn't the most exciting work in the world, but it kept them out of trouble, and they felt they were helping the war effort. Oscy had the better end of the deal, definitely the most interesting part of the work. While Hermie consulted the order sheets, found the items requested, packed and sealed them into boxes, Oscy sat, with shipping label poised, tongue apprized, waiting to paste it on to the box. He refused to work fast and Hermie frequently had to wait until Oscy was thoroughly satisfied with his own effort, before he could move the box on to the freight elevator and make room for the next one. Hermie was very conscientious about everything he did, and it bothered him that Oscy could take everything so lightly. Hermie thought

Oscy was very uncomplicated and he, Hermie, was so complicated. It must be pretty good to be able to let everything float over you without letting it sway you. "There is a war on, Oscy!" "There is? Oh, *that*!" was Oscy's usual attitude. Doctor, to Oscy: "You've got a compound fracture of the tibia and the fibula, Oscy, not to mention the patella and the medulla oblongata." Oscy, to Doctor: "Ah, well, easy come, easy go." "Oscy, the flour's all gone, there'll be no more bread." "Well, that's no problem. Let 'em eat cake," replied Oscy.

A small portable radio was playing in the stockroom. As usual it was pouring out the war report . . . "and this morning Bradley got the favorable weather he was hoping for, and American forces catapulted out of Normandy like the rocket that had been predicted in July . . . and so today, General Omar Bradley commands the greatest U.S. striking force in history, and is now cutting ahead without giving the reeling Germans a chance to recover their balance. In the Pacific the noose continues to tighten and the Japanese can find no way in which to hide from U.S. Airpower. . . ."

Oscy calmly took one of his ready-addressed labels and pasted it over the radio's speaker. Then he switched the radio off.

"What the hell's wrong with you?" asked Hermie.

"I'm sick of news bulletins."

"Do you think if you don't listen it'll maybe go away?"

"I don't give a shit."

"The label's supposed to go on this carton."

"Send 'em the radio."

"I oughta send them you." Just when you'd arrived at the stunning conclusion that the half-naked peasant in his rice-paddy was happier without the joys of civilization. Hermie thought maybe he'd have to revise his estimate of Oscy after all. He gingerly took a hold of the edge of the still-damp label and peeled it away from the speaker.

Now it would need to be taped on to the box. He went over to a drawer to look for tape.

Oscy began tapping his fingers to some inner tune. His whole body responded with a jive movement that made him look like a spastic camel. "Where the hell is Benjie? D'you think he'd leave without saying goodbye?"

Hermie shook his head and concentrated on the label.

"God, I can't believe that kid is going into the Marines. He'll step off the bus at Camp Lejeune, step on a land mine . . . and blow his ass off."

Hermie said nothing. Looking past Oscy he saw Benjie coming into the shipping room through the basement door. Oscy saw Hermie's face and turned too. Benjie was in Marine uniform, and somehow the Supply Sergeant had not received the appropriate specifications for Benjie. The jacket was a bit too big. The pants were baggy and not from the same dye-lot as the jacket. The cap was tilted at just off the right angle. It was Benjie all right, but the uniform had been expertly tailored for someone else . . . a hundred pounds heavier and twelve feet tall. He still looked magnificent. He had a self-conscious grin on his face.

"Mr. Berger said I could come in."

"Goddammit, Benjie . . . you're beautiful." Oscy was really impressed. This made it legal.

"My mother wanted to take a couple of temporary tucks in it, but I couldn't see myself reporting for duty with a lot of threads hanging outta me. My hair goes tomorrow. I have to send it to my mother . . . ain't she something? Well, this is it. I have to catch a Brighton Express." He stood there uncomfortably, not able to take the first step away from them.

Hermie went up to him and took his elbow. "Come on, we'll see you off."

"That'd be very nice."

"Here." Oscy handed Benjie the radio. "A radio. You can keep up with the war."

"No thanks. I expect I'll be living the war." He held awkwardly on to the radio, not knowing what to do with it. Hermie took it from him and put it back on the tool shelf.

"Benjie, you look great. I mean it, you really do. And I envy you. And so does Oscy . . . which is why all his wisenheimer remarks."

Oscy barely acknowledged Hermie's put-down with a smile and slapped Benjie on the back. Hermie led the way. Oscy brought up the rear, admiring Benjie, liking what he saw.

"All right, men!" Oscy brought them to attention. "Our objective is the BMT station! Let's do it for America! By the right! Quick march! Left, right! Left, right! Left, right! Left, left, I had a good home and I left!" They marched out into the street, then turned toward the BMT station, keeping a semblance of rhythm. A couple of kids on the street gaped at Benjie. One crouched behind a trash can and began peppering Benjie with an imaginary machinegun.

"We-you-coming-to-get-Yank," the kid hissed, in a Richard Loo voice. Oscy turned, pulled the pin with his teeth and completely demolished the Jap gun emplacement with a well-aimed pineapple.

"That's one for the Allies," Oscy said, dusting off his hands. The Jap, having given his all and lost, reincarnated himself as an American Marine and tagged along behind Oscy's triumphant platoon, only slightly out of step. The kid's buddy tried to catch up with Benjie and touch him for luck. Benjie tried on a suit of self-assurance, a battle-hardened world-weariness, but he came off looking slightly demented.

Oscy started a new chant, something he'd heard from somebody's brother. "I know a girl who lives on a hill. She won't do it but her sister will. Yes, I know you're right! Yes, I know you're right!" The others joined in, including the kids. "Ain't no sense in looking down,

Ain't no discharge on the ground. Yes, I know you're right! Yes, I know you're right!" It was a victorious platoon that finally reached the BMT station, having downed everything in its path.

They started down the steps to the subway, one-two-three, skip, one-two-three, skip. Needless to report, any other battle accounts to the contrary, Benjie skipped one step too many and almost landed nose first on the turnstile. Righting himself, he faced his two friends.

"Well, this is it," he said again.

Hermie reached behind him and put a nickel in the slot. "It's on me, Benjie. We just never got around to getting you a present."

"Aaaah, it's okay."

"No, it's not. I guess we never really believed you were going. But . . . you're going." For a second Hermie couldn't talk, so he held out his hand. "Take care of yourself, Benjie." He felt a dreadful urge to put his arms around his old friend but knew he couldn't. His throat felt funny, like maybe he was getting a cold.

Oscy pushed Hermie away and slapped Benjie on the back, for good luck. Benjie held out his hand to Oscy. "Oscy, I'll see you. Knock 'em dead, you guys, at Connecticut, okay?"

"Yeah," Oscy sniffed, wiping the back of his hand across his nose. He must be catching Hermie's cold. "Take care of yourself, Benjie."

"I will."

They pulled away from each other and stood gaping through the bars, suddenly worlds apart, not sure which side was the inside of the cage. No one spoke for a minute. There wasn't anything left to say.

Oscy broke the moment. He started rattling the bars and yelling through them like an imprisoned felon. "More privileges! More privileges! I wanna speak to a lawyer!"

Benjie smiled. Oscy would always be Oscy, no matter

what. "I'll drop you both a line, okay? As soon as I find out where I'm headed."

"Send me a samurai sword, will ya, Benjie?" Oscy asked.

"Sure." He pushed his hand through the bars. "Hermie?"

"So long, Benjie." Hermie shook his hand again.

"Oscy?"

"See ya, Benjie." Oscy shook his hand, then stood back to give him an elaborate salute, holding the position as if the Army were passing in review in front of him. Benjie took off down the steps, not turning back again, just flipping off a wave as he turned the corner, out of sight. Hermie and Oscy stood side by side at the bars, like criminals watching freedom disappear on the BMT. After a minute, Oscy said, "Whaddaya think, Hermie?"

"I think he's gonna get off at the wrong station."

"Yeah, he got lost going to Coney Island."

"Twice."

They laughed. Oscy stood looking down the empty stairwell for a second. Hermie turned away and walked up the steps to the street. With a long sigh Oscy gave the bars one farewell shake, like the echo of a revolt, then turned and ran after Hermie.

The sun was shining when they came back to the surface, just as if nothing had happened. They walked along in silence for a few minutes, each wrapped up in his own thoughts.

Oscy, abhorring a vacuum, moved in first. "You believe he's gone? You believe Benjie put on a Marine suit and got on a train and went away? I think it's a Loony Tune."

Hermie didn't answer.

"Listen, Hermie, you haven't said ten words all summer. What the hell is it with you?"

"My mother found us a rooming house near campus."

"Yeah? Well, we're not there yet. One fast subway

ride to Times Square and I'm a goddamned Leather-neck."

"My father wants me to get in at least one year of college. So does yours."

"The war's gonna be over soon!"

"So it'll be over . . . whether you're in it or not."

"Don't you want to go in?"

"Sure I want to go in. But right now it's out of my hands. My father . . ."

"Your father! Your father!" Oscy kicked a can for a good three sewers. "What about your brother-in-law? He's in the war up to his ass! How the hell can you look your sister in the eye?"

"I don't. She's taller than me."

"All right. Be that way. Well, I'll tell ya, Hermie, going into service makes a lot more sense than going to college with a bunch of 4-Fs."

"Well, every man is different." Hermie felt pompous but couldn't stop it. "Each of us has his own road to go."

Oscy, knowing him for years, knew what that was all about. "Oh, that's what you think, eh?"

Hermie relaxed into a smile. "Yeah, I do."

Oscy gave him a playful nudge in the side. Hermie shrugged it off, knowing he deserved it for getting stuffy. Oscy nudged him again, like a big, shaggy sheepdog.

"You go with the wind, eh, boy?" Nudge.

"Yeah."

"Whichever way the wind blows, eh?" Nudge.

"Right."

"Anywhere you hang your hat is home." Nudge.

"Right."

"A new broom sweeps clean." Hermie nudged back.

"A rolling stone gathers no moss." Nudge.

"Too many cooks spoil the bananas." Nudge.

"Then you got it made, man." Nudge.

"Right. Made in the shade." Nudge.

They made their way down the street, caroming off each other like pool balls that hadn't yet learned where the pockets were.

6

Oscy and Hermie were ensconced in their usual booth at Carsten's. Oscy had his feet up on the seat at the side of Hermie. Hermie was picking at a cherry soda, if you can pick at a cherry soda. Oscy looked bored to death and was counting the revolutions of the electric fan in the ceiling as it scythed through the smoke and noise that had tried to escape, but had been stalled for its efforts.

Oscy stopped counting. "Remember how Benjie used to count everything, I mean *time* everything?" He laughed. "I could use his Ingersoll now."

"We didn't hear from him yet, huh?"

"Give him time. He's probably still trying to fight his way out of Coney Island."

"What do you mean? He never was able to even *find* Coney Island."

"Then he's probably still looking for it."

Two very young girls, obviously not out for a brisk constitutional, sauntered by the table. They didn't look

like locals, and had a long time to go before they'd be
old enough to consent. They were both wearing peasant
blouses, low on the shoulder and showing a couple
acres of skin. One had on pedal pushers, with a daisy
embroidered smack in the middle of the crotch. The other
wore a dirndl skirt and crazy wartime wooden wedges.
She looked like Rita Hayworth, from the ankles down.

All that exposed shoulder skin drew Oscy's eyes and
riveted his attention. He whistled his famous mating cry,
for which he was known from Coney Island to Washington Heights. The girls pretended not to hear, but there
was an involuntary wiggle in the peddle pushers that
Oscy was honor-bound to construe as interest. He said,
very loudly, in a dramatic voice, for the girls to hear, "I
fought for this and one day I'm going to see and enjoy
it all."

Hermie shook his head wonderingly. "Where'd you get
that line from?"

"From a Greyhound Bus ad in a magazine. Good
line, huh?"

"Yeah, if you're a bus."

The girls were looking around for an empty table.
Oscar dusted off the seat beside him and put down his
feet. "Uh, ladies, maybe you would do a couple of lonely
servicemen the honor?"

The girls looked at each other and giggled. The one
in the skirt shrugged, almost out of her blouse, which
caused Oscy to rise out of his seat, a formality that wasn't
a regular part of his courting dance, but it helped him see
better, or at least more.

Hermie sighed lightly, but without malice. You couldn't
expect a man to act against his nature just because there
was a war on. "Here we go again, another Woodbury
Deb bites the dust," he said, under his breath.

The girls slid into the booth, Pedal Pushers by Oscy
and Skirt by Hermie. "You guys really in the service?"
Skirt asked, giggling.

"Would I lie?" asked Oscy, his eyebrows shooting up in horror at the very thought. "Alas, my friend here, dear old Doyle, ships out tonight, for Muskogee." He sighed woefully, the horrors of war and parting weighing heavily on his shoulders.

"Where's that?"

"That, my pretty little dears, is where the heaviest fighting is. It's one of the Islands off of Kenosha in the Philippines. You must've heard of it."

"Come to think of it, yes, maybe on the News yesterday" Pedal Pushers was breathlessly impressed. "I'm Jenny. This is Georgia."

"Any relation to the Atlanta Georgias?" asked Oscy, a formality.

Georgia shook her head. These guys talked funny but they looked harmless enough. Anyway, they were in a crowded place.

Oscy introduced Hermie. "My friend, Jim Doyle . . . and I'm Gary . . . Gary Grover."

"Pleased to meet you," said Georgia. "What branch of service are you in?"

"Sshhh!" Oscy cautioned them, and pointed to a poster over his head. It showed a boat going down under fiery bombardment from swastika'd planes. Underneath was printed: LOOSE LIPS SINK SHIPS!

Georgia sucked in her breath. This was the real thing. "OSS?" she mouthed.

"FRD," Oscy breathed, looking around to see if anyone had overheard. Hermie had and was trying hard to hide his laughter in the remains of his cherry soda. FRD stood for Fucka Rubba Duck, one of Oscy's favorite expressions.

"Ooh," said Jenny, wide-eyed.

"Allow me to buy you a drink, a small farewell toast," Oscy begged Georgia.

"Well, maybe a Pepsi, thanks."

"The fair Jenny?"

"Oooh, me too, please." She bit her lip and shrugged at Georgia, intrigued. Georgia moved closer to Hermie, who so far hadn't said a word.

"Doesn't he talk?" she asked Oscy, gesturing to Hermie.

"Ah, maybe I forgot to mention, my friend, poor Doyle, is from the Free French Forces. He speaks no English."

"Georgia knows French. Georgia talk to him in French," Jenny said excitedly.

"Unfortunately, he's from the Polish part of France and only knows Polish." Thank the Lord for that, thought Hermie.

"Perhaps one of you ladies can speak some Polish?"

"I'm afraid not," Georgia apologized, acknowledging her dreadful faux-pas in never having learned it.

"Ah, that's too bad."

Hermie gave Oscar the evil eye, but it didn't land. Oscar continued on, so far into his fantasy that he was beginning to believe it himself. "But I am sure my friend understands and appreciates your good intentions. You are, indeed, lovely ladies." He put his arm around Jenny's shoulders, thereby pushing down the elastic of her peasant blouse to a dangerous level.

The girls glowed, basking in Oscy's gallantry. Oscy knew he had them. He kicked Hermie under the table and gave him the Victory sign. Hermie'd had enough and got up to go. Oscy spoke to him in his own version of Pig Latin. "Whopere opare yopu gopoing?"

"Hopome, thopis opis stopupopid."

"Wope're opin, mopan, dopon't gopo nopow!"

"Oh, God, Oscar," Hermie thought, directing arrows tipped with fury at Oscy. "Won't you ever grow up?"

7

Al was leaving for overseas and Hermie's mother had made a farewell party for him. There was boloney and salami, cold sliced turkey and roast beef, cheese and rye bread, pretzels, olives, pickles, and the two orange layer cakes which'd been in the freezer since Hermie's graduation. There was also an excellent orange-juice punch, into which Hermie suspected his father had sneaked some rum.

The relatives were there, and some of the neighbors. A couple of Ruth's girlfriends buzzed around, trying to help, but Hermie's mother was trying very hard to insure that it would be totally her effort, her farewell to Al, whom she didn't really like, but was trying to persuade everyone she adored.

The party had been going on for almost an hour when Al and Ruth arrived. Al was tousled and tall, obviously a former big-man-on-campus, looking unbearably heroic in his Army officer's uniform. Hermie wondered why it was that people like Al always got uniforms that fit and people like Benjie always got uniforms that didn't. Ruth looked hollow-eyed, as if she hadn't slept for a week. The skin across her cheeks was drum-tight, her nose suspiciously red at the tip. She stayed very close to Al, not letting him out of her sight for a second. Everybody very carefully avoided mentioning the reason for the party. It might have been a continuation of the graduation party.

Aunt Nell fussed around Al, fluffing up the cushion in back of his chair, bringing him sandwiches and cake, punch, cookies. Hermie's mother finally dragged her away, saying, "Leave the boy alone. You'll make him sick." Then she descended on Al, under the staggering weight of a blue-iced cake with a Marine on top. "You like it? I made it," she announced.

Ruth laughed. "Al's in the Army, Mom, not the Marines."

"Army, Marines, what's the difference? It's all soldiers."

"There is a difference, Mother."

Al could feel Ruth was ready to fight. It was something that only came on when she was around her mother. The Army should bottle up some of that tension and use it against the enemy. Would that Zap the Jap! He squeezed her elbow, meaning "Don't fight. Not now." She relaxed and rubbed herself a little closer into his side.

Most people were trying hard not to talk about the war, or fighting, or soldiers, or leaving home. There were so many forbidden subjects that the room was littered with dead air at regular intervals, when only busily chewing jaws could be heard. Then, in embarrassment, someone would jump into the breach with an inane remark.

"Well, I guess it'll soon be time for you to be cracking the books, Hermie?" Uncle Nat gave him a protective pat on the back.

Hermie looked over to Al to see if he'd heard. Al seemed to be engrossed in memorizing the shape of the fingers on Ruth's left hand.

"I was thinking of going up into New York State and maybe working on one of the farms up there." Hermie hadn't thought of it until just that minute, but it seemed like a nice patriotic thing to do. "Just until September."

"But you're working in Harlan's Drug House." His mother had heard through the tumult and two closed doors. "It's a good job. You don't have to leave home so fast. Your mother shouldn't have to worry." She filled up Hermie's plate. "Here, eat." As far as anyone was concerned, that settled it. Defeated, Hermie returned to a corner where he could contemplate his life uninterrupted. That is, if his mother let him.

Al finally broke the awful silence himself. "Look, you don't have to treat me like a leper. What I've got isn't catching. I'm going overseas, that's all." He put his arm around Ruth and squeezed, obviously pressing the right button, because the tears started coursing down her cheeks. "Listen, folks, I want to read something to you. Maybe it'll explain why I feel I gotta go."

Everyone stopped talking. Hermie's mother stopped filling up people's plates. Ruth sat very still at Al's side. He took a piece of paper out of his pocket and prepared to read from it. No one moved. Glasses and cups were still. The coffee perked self-consciously in the kitchen. Ruth held on to Al's arm as he began.

"This is from an essay, written by a man who was wounded . . . a Brooklyn man." He looked around. "It's a bit the way I feel, only I'm not too good at words. This is it. 'I fight because of my memories—the laughter and play of my childhood, the ball games I was in, the better ones I watched, my mother telling me why my father and she came to America, my high school graduation, the first time I saw a cow, the first year we could afford a vacation, hikes in the fall, weenie and marshmellow roasts, the first time I voted, my first date and the slap in the face I got instead of the kiss I attempted, the El going down, streets being widened to let the sun in, new tenements replacing the old slums, the crowd applauding the time I came through with the hit that won us the Borough championship—the memories which, if people like me do not fight for, our children will never have.' "

There was silence in the room, broken only by a couple of sniffles from Aunt Tess and Ruth, who was openly crying.

To hide her feelings, Hermie's mother adopted her usual tone of semi-anger. "Now, look what you've done," she reproached her son-in-law.

"That's all right, Mom," Ruth sniffled. "I'm not unhappy. I'm proud. And I wish you'd all stop treating this like it was some kind of sacred moment. Just pretend it's Thanksgiving or Christmas or something. Men go off to work. Men go off to war. . . ." She rushed out of the room and Al followed her, kind of wordlessly apologizing to the company as he left. Everyone shuffled uncomfortably for a couple of seconds.

The conversation soon picked up. It wasn't easy to be unhappy for too long. Uncle Nat grumbled about his A gasoline card, and Aunt Tess bemoaned the quality of Grade C beef, which was cheaper, but oh, so stringy. They talked about Mrs. Dumont down the street who had three blue stars in her window, and about Benjie's mother, who'd stuffed a cushion with his curls.

Ruth came back in, looking kissed, and Al went over to the phonograph and put on "Paper Doll." He held out his arms and they swayed dreamily in front of the phonograph as the conversation weaved around them.

"Whaddaya think of that Mel Ott? 483 home runs! 1,749 runs batted in! And he's thirty-five years old! Me, I couldn't swing a bat to beat the Axis."

"I'm gonna buy a paper doll,
    That I can call my own.
    A doll that other fellas cannot steal . . ."

"Read about the guy who used up his last gas coupons to fill up his tank, then his four-year old son came along and filled up the rest of the tank with water and vitamin pills?"

"There's a new insecticide, DDT it's called. Spray it on a wall, it kills any fly that touches the wall for up to three months after."

"They should spray it in Hitler's urinal."

"Yes, I love you, and that's why I have to go."

"I know, Al, I just wish it was all over."

"Can we get out of here now without offending your mother? I'm leaving in two hours and there's something I have to tell you."

"Tell me now."

"Unh-uh, not here, baby. We'd be arrested."

Ruth giggled. "All right . . . let's sneak out through the kitchen."

Hermie saw them going. He called his mother over. "Hey, Ma, you got any more of that cake?" She came running over with alacrity, and the cake. She didn't notice the back screen door slam as Ruth and Al left.

Hermie sat in the corner and stuffed his face with cake he didn't want. He didn't feel as if he were part of anybody's world.

8

On June 22nd Hermie and Oscy worked in the shipping room of Harlan's Wholesale Drugs. On June 26th the Japanese mainland was attacked for the first time by U.S. B-29 Super-Fortress bombers. On June 26th Oscy and Hermie spent the afternoon doing nothing in Prospect Park. On June 27th General Charles de Gaulle returned to his native France. On July 1st Hermie and Oscy pretended they weren't crying as they watched "Since You Went Away" at the Avalon. On July 3rd Tom Dewey became candidate for President for the Republican party. On July 10th Oscy and Hermie searched through the summer crop of girls at Brighton Beach. On July 13th General Tojo resigned. On July 19th Hermie and Oscy sat in Carsten's, their ears blasted by Frankie and Bing and Sammy Kaye and The Duke. On July 24th FDR announced that he would run for a fourth term. On July 30th Oscy and Hermie threw a lethargic ball to each other on Avenue P. On July 31st an attempt was made on the life of Hitler by some of the most trusted members of his General Staff. On August 28th Hermie and Oscy lay in the sun in Prospect Park, frying their brains and not listening to the baseball game on the radio. On September 4th Paris was freed. On September 5th Oscy and Hermie walked nonchalantly into a bar on Ocean Parkway, and just as nonchalantly were escorted out by a beefy Irishman. On September 18th the lights went on again in London.

On September 19th Oscy and Hermie prepared for college by having one last soda at Carsten's.

"Y'know, Hermie, who Sad Sack reminds me of?" Oscy said. "Benjie."

"Yeah," Hermie answered, "see the cartoon where he was measured for his uniform and it ended up being ten times too big for him?"

"Wonder how Benjie's doing?"

"Yeah."

Oscy was flipping through a magazine. "Y'know what it says here?" he asked Hermie, and without waiting for an answer, began reading. " Sometimes a recruit, being examined by psychiatrists is truculent, has a chip-on-the-shoulder attitude. Navy psychiatrists have learned by experience that such a recruit is not necessarily a psychiatric personality unfit for service; he may be a perfectly normal guy from Brooklyn. Says the *N.Y. State Journal of Medicine*; the Navy doctors have christened this harmless social pattern the 'Brooklyn Syndrome'."

Hermie laughed and shrugged. "I always thought we were members of an underdeveloped nation."

"Hey, do you think I have the 'Brooklyn Syndrome', Hermie?" Oscy stood over Hermie with his fist raised as if to strike. "Do you?"

Hermie ducked. "No, Oscy, you're the very picture of an untruculent guy, on my life."

"All right then," said Oscy, relaxing.

*　　　*　　　*

It was a long summer.

Hermie listened to Dooley Wilson sing "As Time Goes By," and danced with Ingrid Bergman as Humphrey Bogart, in trenchcoat, looked on.

Oscy, in an old raincoat of his father's and a battered derby hat, spied on the enemy in the schoolyard of PS 84.

Hermie saw "Going My Way" twice at the Fox, and cried with the rest of the audience when Barry Fitzgerald was united with his aged mother.

Oscy, surrounded by admiring girls in Carsten's, told them of his exploits in the Libyan desert.

Hermie lined up for tickets outside the Paramount to see Frank Sinatra, and imagined himself mobbed by gorgeous females as they mistook him for "The Voice."

Paulie Marcus' sister, in hysterical tears, came into Hermie's house and showed his mother a telegram from the War Department. Hermie's mother turned off the roast in the oven and rushed over to the Marcus house without even stopping to throw on a sweater.

It was a long summer.

9

Hermie was ready to go to school. He was packed. His mother had seen to that. He had on a shirt and tie, and pants with a crease. His valise sat expectantly on a chair, waiting for the final closing. Hermie looked around the room. It looked like a kid's room. There was a teddy bear, long ago discarded, but still sitting up on a shelf, baseballs and a football, a picture of Penny Singleton, no longer his idol, but he'd pasted the photo to the wall and couldn't get it off without leaving a tear in the wallpaper. There was another picture of Bing Crosby from "Going My Way." There was a "No Exit" sign that he and Oscy had "borrowed" from Yankee Stadium, and a Pretty Girl from Esquire that he'd drawn a mustache on, in the wrong place. A Model-T that he'd put together from a kit was hanging from the lightbulb, and the sign over the bed said "No Parking Please." His old saddleshoes were peeking out from under the bed. He decided to leave them there. It made the room look as if someone lived there.

It was a funny thing about going to college. Once you left for school, that was it, you no longer lived at home. Home wasn't really your home any more. You could come for visits. Your mother was still your mother. But the house you'd lived in all those years wasn't ever going to be home again in the same way. First college, then a job, or the Army, then marriage, probably. But that room that had seen so many triumphs and failures, fantasies and real-life dramas, private moments and masturbations, victories and defeats, tears and joys, frustrations and exhilarations, was really like an extended womb that had outlived its usefulness. This was the last time he could really call it home. He didn't think his mother really appreciated this, or she'd have been in there weeping all over the place. Or maybe she did and that's why she wasn't, because Mothers learned to accept that things changed and children grew up and went away. His room had been a very private place, but it wasn't really his any more. He'd heard that some mothers even rented rooms out to boarders when sons went off to college. Hermie didn't think he'd like that. But then he couldn't really lay claim to it any more. It was open territory. Only the memories belonged to him.

The thing was, of course, to take your memories with you, since they had no meaning for anyone else. But you had to have somewhere to store them and that was why people had to have rooms of their own, or houses, he supposed. Some things he didn't want to remember, but they were there too. He'd have to set aside separate drawers, carefully labelled, for those things he wished he could forget, like when his dog died, and the awful time he'd laid a fart right in the middle of Mr. Zucker's Ancient History class. He'd pretended it came from the Chemistry Lab next door and made some loud comments about Chemistry freaks trying to blow up the world. It hadn't worked, because everybody knew, and Oscy had chalked it up against him on his imaginary scoreboard, very elaborately writing in the air "H" and "1." The best thing about those kind of memories was that nobody else remembered them any more, so they were a bit like excess baggage that should have been left behind.

Hermie wondered what happened to old memories when somebody died. Who cleaned them out and threw them away. He remembered a scary movie or a story, he wasn't sure which, about a mirror that stored memories and played back scenes from the room's past to its present occupants. That's probably what ghosts were, if there were such things, just old, bad memories come back to try and be important again.

He tried to think about dying. He lay very still on his bed and tried to feel dead. You had to think of nothing, which was practically impossible, because the more you thought about nothing, the more some new thought would crowd in and drown out your nothing. Instead of thinking of nothing at all, which was too hard, he thought about how the people he knew would take his dying. His parents would weep a lot and Oscy and Benjie would be given compassionate leave to come home and mourn for him. His sister sobbed on the window seat and Hermie felt so sorry for himself that the tears came to his own eyes. That reminded him he wasn't dead. Then he wondered what he would feel like if Benjie were killed, or Al, or Oscy. He couldn't really picture them dead, because he wasn't the main character. Oscy and Benjie'd have to do their own imagining. Hermie liked the idea of everybody crying over him. It would probably be the only time in his life or, rather, death, he'd ever be the real center of attention.

Maybe he better do a few more things before he died, though. He'd hate to be dying and wondering what it might have been like to go to college, or get married, or make a baby, or watch his son graduate, or be decorated by President Roosevelt, or ride the cable-cars in San Francisco, or ski in the Austrian Alps, or single-handedly sail around the world, or write a book, or kill three Japs with one shot of his .45 caliber Thompson submachine gun, or be the sole survivor after thirty days on a raft in the North Atlantic.

The sea was icy cold, hostile around them in its steely blackness. Not the sight or sound of a ship, a bird, a floating spar to break the awful, ominous blackness. He'd given the last drop of water from his canteen to his rear-gunner, who had passed out now on the raft, one hand trailing in the glacial ocean. He reached over and pulled the man's hand back onto the raft, to avoid attracting the attention of hungry sharks. As he touched his buddy's hand, he felt its clammy stiffness and knew . . . what he did not want to know. For three hours he didn't move, just sat and stared at the lifeless body of the man who had been his friend. The rolling of the waves had moved the body, so that it was half off, half on the raft. As dawn came up over the horizon, he knew what he had to do if he were to survive. With his boot he reached over and gently tipped his pal into the bubbling sea. "Goodbye, old friend," he said. "It was a short life, but it was good while it lasted." As he turned to face the sun that was already casting its life-giving rays over the raft, he seemed to feel the boards beneath him speed up, and realized that he was being drawn by the tide into the shores of what seemed to be a beautiful tropical island. The palm trees waved gently in the morning breeze and a group of dark-haired, bare-breasted wahinis were wading out into the ocean to bring him to land.

Suddenly the raucous sound of a car horn shattered his dream. He jumped up and looked out of the window. There was a cab in front of the house, and leaning over the cabbie and onto the horn, was Oscy, impatient as ever.

Hermie's mother came running to his bedroom door. "Hermie, the cab's here. It's time to go. Do you have everything packed? I knew I should've done it for you." She clapped her hand to her head.

"It's all right, Ma, it's all packed." Hermie felt a spasm of affection for her. She only recognized her own existence when she was worrying. He put his arm around her shoulders and she leaned against him for a second.

"Hermie . . . little Hermie," she sighed, which made no logical sense, because he towered over her a good head and shoulders.

"I'm only going to Connecticut, Ma. I'll be home for Thanksgiving."

"I know, I know. Go already. Oscy'll break the horn yet." He let her kiss him, bending so she could reach his cheek. "Be a good boy, now. An honor to your parents. We should be proud."

His father tapped at the door and opened it. "Your bags ready, Hermie?" Hermie nodded. His father went over to the suitcase and closed up the lid, sitting on it at the last moment to get it to fasten. He took the suitcase, and the overnighter that Hermie'd already closed, and carried them both down the stairs and out to the cab. Hermie and his mother followed. Hermie noticed, for the first time, that his father had a spot on the top of his head where the hair was rapidly thinning. It was carefully concealed.

Hermie's mother held back her tears. She pushed something into Hermie's pocket and patted it to make sure it couldn't fall out. Oscy stopped leaning on the horn when he saw Hermie's father in the vanguard of the little procession, for which the cabbie was truly grateful.

"You'll write, Hermie." It was a command, not a question.

"I'll call, Ma. I'll be within spitting distance." Hermie threw his suitcases into the cab.

"You shouldn't forget your manners your mother taught you. Remember, you're still a Green."

"Yeah, Ma, I'll remember." Hermie gave her a perfunctory peck on the cheek, then held out his hand to his father. His father took his hand in both of his, then shook it and nodded his head. He didn't say anything. Hermie felt the familiar crackle of a straight-from-the-bank bill as his father withdrew his hands. There'd never been an important occasion when this little ceremony hadn't been performed. Hermie couldn't think of anything to say, so he turned and climbed into the cab, having to step over Oscy, who insisted on remaining at the left side of the back seat.

"Come on, Hermie. I been waiting twenty cents worth on the fuckin' meter." Oscy grumbled. "Okay, Speedy, we can go now."

The cabbie took off in a burst of speed that was a more-than-adequate statement. Hermie shot back into the seat and was only able to right himself in time to catch a last glimpse of his parents, small in the distance and growing smaller as the cab turned the corner.

"Christ," Oscy complained, "we can blow our whole tuition money just waiting around."

Hermie sighed, having caught his breath. "Well, there they go."

Oscy looked at him as if he were crazy.

10

On the train Oscy and Hermie sat opposite each other, not talking. Hermie was deep into a book. Oscy was drawing tits on the steamy window. The train was unduly crowded, mostly sailors heading for New London, or other Connecticut military bases. Oscy had had enough of Hermie's silence. "What the hell're you reading?" he asked.

"The cheers. Songs and cheers for football games."

"You're kidding!"

"You asked."

"You gonna wear a chrysanthemum, too?"

"Shut up, Oscy."

Oscy shut up, for the space of about twenty railroad ties, the longest Oscy ever shut up. Then he said, "This should be a troop train. Every time I see a serviceman ... We should be reading Army Field Manuals, not learning cheers. I give this school two weeks." Getting no response from Hermie, he tried another tack. "I expect you to know four cheers and a marching song within the hour, Joe College."

Hermie didn't look up. "One of the main reasons you'll never be in the Army, Oscy, is that you're *already* Section Eight."

Oscy made a face, indicating that was all right with him.

Hermie looked over at him. "Do you ever listen to yourself?"

Oscy looked out of the window and began drumming on the glass, at the spot where his steam-filled tits were fading out of existence. "No. I got better things to do." He liked that and laughed, repeating it a couple of times.

Nothing had ever been or ever would be like a train in wartime. A train used to be a means of going from place A to place B. But now it had a whole new significance. There was an increased urgency to the chuff of the everyday engine, and the whistle had accepted for itself a self-importance that only previously belonged to campaign trains, or those carrying diplomats, or exotic potentates on royal missions. This train, going into Connecticut, had its share of important cargo on board. Sailors going off to sail, soldiers going off to fight, girls going to meet their men for an illicit weekend on a forty-eight hour pass, mothers going to wave goodbye to sons they might never see again, families of servicemen, the kids lollipopped into sticky sleep, going to move into temporary quarters near the barracks, to be close when the overseas orders came.

Hermie felt his own mission should've been more important. He was taking up valuable space. He looked around the compartment, trying to spot a German spy. But there was only an old farmer, traveling home with his new government permits; an old woman with a baby granddaughter on her lap, who had confided to Hermie that the mother of the child had run off with a Marine and she was the one who had to go to break the news to her son, who was shipping out for Europe; a young couple who were obviously lost to everything except each other; two soldiers, one bursting out of his buttons, the other so thin he could be used to clean out the cannon. And Oscy, whom no one in his right mind would ever entrust with secret information. A secret given to Oscy had the life-span of about forty-six seconds, and that only if he had his mouth full at the time you told it to him.

A vendor walked down the aisle, hawking his goodies. Hermie wondered if he might be a spy, but in the old Orient Express movies the spy always looked like Peter Lorre, and this vendor looked more like Mickey Rooney.

"Baby Ruths, chewing gum, O'Henrys . . . peanut butter crackers, orange drink . . . Coca-Cola," the Vendor called from side to side as he fought his way down the crowded aisle.

Oscy stopped him. "Any Connecticut cheers?"

"All out," the Vendor said, automatically.

"Hey, Hermie," Oscy said, hitting his knee, "give the man one of your cheers." Hermie handed him the booklet.

"Do it yourself," he said.

"Rah-rah-rah . . ."

"Sis-boom-bah." Oscy yelled out.

"That'll be 15¢," Oscy told the Vendor.

"Up yours," said the Vendor, with an appropriate gesture, and continued on.

"D'you think he might be a German spy?" Oscy asked Hermie.

"No, I already checked him out. His teeth-braces were made in Detroit," said Hermie.

"Damn," said Oscy.

"Baby Ruths, chewing gum, O'Henrys . . . peanut butter crackers, orange drinks, Coca-Cola . . ." called out the Vendor again, in exactly the same rhythm as he continued down the train.

"I wonder how many years it took him to graduate grade school," Oscy pondered. Bored, he started leafing through the booklet. "Does it say here that there's twenty girls for every man, and that it's our patriotic duty to keep those girls properly serviced so that when the boys come home they won't get tetanus because the girls are rusty? Hey, Hermie, you're in one of your world-famous death-like trances. One of these days they'll cart you off and you'll never know it."

Hermie sighed. "I'm just more selective than you. You're the most undiscriminating guy I know. You'll screw anything that moves."

"You'd better believe it. Did you read where that old guy said university life'd be better for everybody if university students had temporary childless marriages?"

"What old guy?"

"Bernard Russell . . . something like that."

"Who's he?"

"How should I know. You're the brain. Probably plays first base for the Giants."

"You probably mean Lord Bertrand Russell, nitwit, and he doesn't play first base for anyone."

"Not athletic, huh?"

"He's about three hundred years old, idiot."

"Ah, that explains it."

"Explains what?"

"Why he couldn't make the team."

Hermie turned away and looked out of the window.

"You'll probably still be making your selection when you're 93, the rate you're going," Oscy said.

"We'll see," said Hermie.

"Not me. I don't want to miss a single one." Oscy thumbed through the college booklet. "Fraternities. They've got fraternities. Big deal. Only fraternity I'm interested in is Feela Betta Thigh." He nudged Hermie. "Get it? Get it?"

"I got it. I got it."

"Then squeeze it. Squeeze it. It's all part of my over-all philosophy."

"They'll probably publish it. Oscy's Philosophy."

"They should. Wanna hear it?" He didn't wait for Hermie to answer. "If there's a war, get in. If there's a girl, get in. If there's trouble . . . get out." He nudged Hermie again. "Keep that foremost in your mind, my good man."

"I will. I will."

11

The boys found Mrs. Gilhuly's rooming house without any trouble. It was close to campus and had probably seen generations of students come and go. Hermie's mother had come up and picked it out for them, so Hermie knew it'd have the two chief requirements for living, according to the Gospel of Hermie's Mother—lots of food and plenty of hot water, for bathing, of course. Mrs. Gilhuly was so much like his mother in shape and general attitude, she could have been a long lost sister stolen away at birth by Irish leprechauns and brought up in a foreign place.

"There are six other students living here," Mrs. Gilhuly told them as she led the way to their room. "Respect their privacy and they will respect yours. The bathroom is down the hall. No baths after ten o'clock."

Oscy nodded at the end of each sentence as if he were really listening and recording all her instructions. With strangers he always came off as an admirable boy, so charming, such gentlemanly behavior! "You'll find clean towels in your room," Mrs. Gilhuly continued. "There's a pay phone on the first landing. No incoming calls after ten o'clock." They had reached their room. Mrs. Gilhuly opened the door and led the way in. She busied herself opening windows, fluffing up pillows, opening closet doors. The room smelled of mothballs and Lysol. "There's storage space in the basement. You can keep your trunks down there. No one's allowed in the basement after ten o'clock."

"Ten o'clock's really witching hour around here, isn't it?" whispered Oscy. "Something must've happened to her once at ten o'clock!"

Hermie sshh'd him. Oscy wrinkled his nose at the strong smell of disinfectant in the room. "Probably had to scrub the last tenants off the walls," Oscy whispered.

Mrs. Gilhuly turned and gave Hermie a look. She wasn't sure which of them had spoken, but she'd known enough students to be able to read *that* one at a glance. "Breakfast is between seven and eight on weekdays; between eight and ten on weekends. No food will be served after ten o'clock on Sunday mornings."

"Again with the ten o'clock," hissed Oscy.

"Three ration coupons per boy per meal, payable in advance. Well, Oscar and Herman," she said, standing back, her hands on her broad hips, finished with the guided tour. "I wish you good luck at Connecticut University."

Together, Oscy and Hermie answered, "Thank you."

Mrs. Gilhuly went out, leaving the door open a crack. Oscy quickly closed it and plopped himself down on the bed nearest the window. Mrs. Gilhuly poked her nose back into the room and aimed directly at Hermie, right between the eyes. "And no girls in the rooms!" She withdrew and Hermie looked at Oscy.

"Why me?"

"I guess you have the look of the lecher, old fellow,"

said Oscy. "She liked me. You know who she reminded me of?"

Hermie nodded his head in agreement.

"Your mother's missing identical twin. Right here! Utterly fantastic."

"Any preference on the beds?" Hermie asked.

"Nope," said Oscy amiably, but he'd already unfastened his suitcase and had its contents spread out over the bed by the window.

"Right," said Hermie, plopping on the other bed. "I'll take this one."

"Good idea," said Oscy, scattering his personal equipment over bed, bureau and floor. "How does one get a girl up here? It's three floors up and a sheer drop into a bottomless pit."

"You could try letting down your hair, like Rapunzel," said Hermie. "Anyway, no girls allowed. You heard from the Oracle."

"She was talking to you, not me. I don't look the type. I'm the type any mother could trust. Anyway, I always say, the Lord takes care of those who take care of themselves. That's what I always say." He assumed a prayerful attitude. Throwing some of his clothes into a drawer, not overly concerned with tidiness, he continued his thought. "If I find a girl I like, I'm gonna fit her up with suction cups and leave the window unlocked."

"I still think you should let down your hair."

Oscy, bored with unpacking, threw the last of his things into the bottom of the closet. "Come on, let's take a stroll on campus and see what this college shit is all about."

"Shouldn't we unpack first?"

"I already unpacked."

"That's unpacked?" Hermie looked at Oscy's clothes on the floor of the closet.

"Look, if I'd wanted my mother with me, I'd've brought her. Don't be an old lady, Hermie. The truth is, I don't

know if I'm staying. If this school isn't everything I've
ever dreamed of . . . if Linda Darnell isn't the head cheer-
leader and if Jack Oakie doesn't make five touchdowns
against Pottowatamie, then I'm gathering up my ration
coupons and I'm transferring my ass to Dartmouth.
Father or no father."

Hermie shrugged. "Lead on, McOscar." They closed
the door carefully after them, so as not to encourage any
snooping by the mother substitute allotted to them, and
started out for the campus.

"Hermie, remember that cheer you learned on the way
up? How did it go?"

"Rah-rah-rah . . .

Sis-boom-bah!" said Hermie.

"Right, let's go!" Oscy took Hermie's arm and they
walked off down the street, rah-rahing, sis-boom-bahing,
Hermie very quietly, Oscy very loudly.

They'd been given the guided tour when they came
up for their interviews, but now that they were here as
students it looked quite different. Buildings they'd thought
were in one place had changed location and surfaced
someplace else. The campus looked enormous and very
threatening, as if daring them to even plumb its depths.
Hermie'd been told that in peacetime there were almost
eight thousand students. Of course, with many of the men
away, it was probably coed heaven now, except for the
Hermies and Oscars.

Hermie and Oscy found themselves under the same
microsopic consideration that they were extending to their
fellow students. 4-Fs or fags? seemed to be the scientific
question. They tried to storm through the campus like
visiting Huns, to leave no doubt in anyone's minds that
they fell into neither of the former categories. Oscy
noticed the girls and Hermie commented on the architec-
ture. On one thing they were in agreement; there was no
shortage of gargoyles.

The town, like any other town, was bedecked with wartime posters. Otherwise it could've been any town, any time in the twentieth century. There were stores and church yards, bars and restaurants, drug stores and service stations, soda shops, parks, mothers and babies, library, town hall, people who looked like people everywhere. A couple of soldiers on furlough, the inevitable girls clutching their arms.

"Maybe we could rent some uniforms," said Oscy.

"Looks like any other town," said Hermie.

"Seen one you've seen 'em all," said Oscy. "We've done the tour. The girls all look like bulldogs. Let's go."

They strolled back to Mrs. Gilhuly's, neither one making scintillating conversation. Hermie tried to project himself forward about two months to when the whole place would be so familiar that it'd feel like home. New places always did that to you, made you feel sort of useless.

But after a few days you couldn't remember when it'd seemed new to you, and everything seemed just as familiar as your own front stoop. Meanwhile they could have been on Mars. Suppose a fire broke out in that department store just as they were walking past it, Hermie wouldn't even know where the Fire Station was, or the Police Station, or even the nearest phone booth. He couldn't be of the slightest assistance, except in going in and dragging out the charred bodies of youngsters who'd been separated from their mothers. Again and again he'd go in, with no thought for his own safety. He saw in detail the pretty girl who was wetting handkerchieves for him to put over his nose and mouth as he once more braved the fiery furnace. Only the smile on her face, a mixture of pride and love, gave Hermie the courage to go back in, racking up an unbelievable total of twenty-five lives saved. He refused to give his name to the scores of clamoring newshounds as he walked down the street, his clothes in tatters, his hair singed, his hands scarred. The lovely Lady of the Handkerchieves, her dress torn to reveal her perfect breasts, waved sadly, a brave smile on her trembling lips as he walked out of her life and right on to Oscy's heels.

Hermie apologized.

"What the fuck!" screamed Oscy. "Whyn't you look where you're going!" Truth was, Oscy had been concentrating very hard on the bouncy walk of a pony-tailed coed just ahead. He'd almost gotten it down pat, and was about to move in when Hermie trod on his heel. The girl turned around when Oscy yelled. He saw her face for the first time. He was glad he hadn't caught up with her. She looked like Walt Disney's Goofy. They went back to Mrs. Gilhuly's for supper, Hermie wondering why his fantasies always ended with bare-breasted women, and Oscy wondering why girls who looked so great from the back could look like such dogs from the front.

The six other students at Mrs. Gilhuly's were, needless to say, all of the male persuasion, although there was one Oscy thought wouldn't take much persuading to try something else. There was one rotund type who exerted a kind of baronial influence over the others. He had an older man's portliness and was losing his hair fast. He lost a good deal of it into his soup that very night.

The Baron mumbled a grace before the meal and in the same breath demanded food coupons from each of the boys present. When he'd collected them, he presented them on a plate to Mrs. Gilhuly, who was waiting at the kitchen door for them, before she would serve the meal. The Baron gave a sort of half bow as he handed her the plate. Oscy whispered in Hermie's ear, "He's making it with your mother's twin. I know the look."

Hermie tended to agree. It was like a ritual that had been worked out over the months. Mrs. Gilhuly bowed slightly as she accepted the plate. Maybe she and the Baron were in cahoots to bilk the boys of their ration coupons, then planned to sail away to some fabulous desert isle where they'd live happily ever after on the proceeds of their sale of the coupons to rich bankers who were stockpiling in case of siege.

The meal was scarcely a three-coupon meal, consisting of a watery soup, a tuna-and-noodle casserole, with more noodle than tuna, and a jello mold in the shape of a land mine, which ran out before it reached Hermie. There were some scrubby radishes and scallions in the middle of the table, and a giant cucumber with a case of terminal acne. Mrs. Gilhuly proudly announced that the vegetables were courtesy of Jeff's Victory Garden, which she'd allowed him to plant in the back yard. Jeff turned out to be the Baron. Oscy turned to Hermie and nodded his head. "Wonder what time *he* has to have lights out? Bet it's not ten o'clock." No one seemed willing to sample the vegetables.

12

Hermie and Oscy went to get their books for the semester at the college bookstore. Oscy was down in the dumps, not at all thrilled at the action in college. "So far, what has it been . . . three days? Well, I'm unimpressed. Outside of one redhead with teeth like a Jap general . . . and *she* asked if I was on the football team. I'm totally unimpressed."

"Try out for the football team. You'll make 'it' and 'her'," Hermie suggested.

"The football team is made up of 4-Fs and homos. If I'm gonna carry the ball for old Connecticut U, I gotta have better blocking than that."

"Maybe they could make it a coed team," Hermie suggested, pointing at a particularly buxom rear bending over the Solid Geometry section.

"Hermie, you don't know anything. I can see I'm going to have to take you in hand."

"Oscy, you've been trying for eighteen years. Give up already."

"It's never too late, Hermie. You can be redeemed. Let's go get a soda. I get a psychosomatic stomachache in book shops."

"You *are* a psychosomatic stomachache, Oscy. I'll meet you there after I've got all my books."

"God, Hermie, the way you carry on, anyone'd think you came to college to *study!*"

Oscy took off, whistling "Coming in on a Wing and a Prayer" very loudly, to the horror of the matronly man who was trying to run the bookstore like a library reading-room.

The next time Hermie saw Oscy he was in a school corridor, trying to make headway with a coed. Oscy had followed her the length of the corridor and was just about to knock up against her so that her books would fall out of her arms. Hermie watched with interest. The girl was cute, with a checkered skirt and a light blue sweater pulled way down over her hips. Oscy made his move, but misjudging her weight, slid and fell heavily to the floor as she tottered slightly and moved out of his way. She bent down and asked him if he was all right. Oscy, red in the face, and not at all pulled-together, asked if he could be of any assistance.

"I think you're the one who needs assistance," she giggled, tossing her curls, just as an ox-like basketball type came dribbling around the corner and literally commandeered the girl, dragging her books from under her arm and almost sweeping her off her feet as they swung away, down the corridor and into oblivion.

Oscy sat on the floor for a couple of minutes, contemplating his navel, not to mention the ludicrousness of his position.

Hermie skidded up. "May I be of some assistance, young man?" he asked.

Oscy threw *Canterbury Tales* at him, doing nothing for

the appearance of the book. It was such an old copy it was probably a first folio. Now, however, its value had been seriously diminished. Oscy's comment, as Hermie, oh so gallantly, helped him to his feet, was rudimentary.

The two boys walked off down the corridor, Oscy slightly subdued, Hermie still amused.

"This place is a jinx on me," Oscy grumbled.

"Maybe if you didn't try so hard," said Hermie.

"What the hell do you know?" Oscy was still mad at himself. "A fraternity expressed an interest in me this morning."

"Which one?"

"I dunno. They got such stupid names. I think it was Fucka Rubba Duck."

"You should know how to do that."

"I have to check out their dining room. My brother says it's the only way to select a fraternity . . . the *food*."

"Well, anything'd be better than our boarding house."

"Hey, when do you think she and the Baron plan to make their dastardly move?"

"Maybe at ten o'clock tonight."

"Can you imagine that combination . . . naked?" Oscy shuddered.

"Don't make me sick. Maybe we can pledge for the same fraternity," said Hermie.

"That'll be one of my conditions. Take me, take my friend," Oscy said staunchly.

"I don't think it works quite like that," said Hermie.

Oscy was making no attempt to study. He was face down on his bed with a copy of *Esquire*. "You know, I can't think why they stopped them from sending these through the mail to our boys."

"It was something to do with morale."

"What's morals got to do with morale?"

"What're you asking me? I'm not the Post Master General," Hermie said, trying to get back to his studying.

After a while Oscy rolled over and threw his copy of *Esquire* out the window. "You say something?" he asked Hermie.

"No."

"Must've been the wind. The wind does funny things in the tropics."

"I'm giving thought to the school newspaper." Herm had done some writing in high school and thought journalism might be something he could be interested in. Most people went out for something, and except for running a bit, he didn't feel a particular interest in any of the sports. Football was out of the question. He wasn't tall enough for basketball. And curb ball wasn't terribly popular in college. Besides, he felt most sports were a bit of a waste of time. He could see where some people got their identity through sports, but he preferred a more solid base, like a desk and a chair, and maybe a typewriter.

"The school newspaper, huh? Yeah, you do that," Oscy said. "Sell enough, maybe you'll get a bicycle."

Hermie tried to read his English assignment. From Oscy's side of the room came a series of enormous sighs, in pattern, three short, one long, four short, two long, three short, one long.

Hermie glared over at Oscy. "All right, keep it up, Oscy."

"Ah, I see the beautiful composure shattered by an offhand sigh. It's reaching you, eh?"

Hermie closed his book with a bang. "*You're* reaching me. I can't study with you around. You don't shut up, not for a minute."

"Oh?"

"Yeah . . . 'oh'. One week out of Brooklyn and you go berserk."

"Now, that's not true. Hermie. I've always been berserk. You just never noticed it in my natural habitat."

"Well, I have noticed that I seem to be sharing a room

with the werewolf of London." Hermie picked up his books and started for the door.

Oscy slowly began to change into a wolf. "Agggg . . . yaggggh . . . help me, doctor." He plopped on to the floor and began writhing around in his metamorphosis. The hair slowly began to cover his forehead and his finger nails grew into long, pointy claws. Two fangs had suddenly found their way through his upper lip and were descending ominously as his body slowly, slowly changed into that of Lon Chaney. "Yaggga-aaggaaahh!" The room was no longer big enough for the both of them. Hermie coolly opened the door and started out.

Suddenly the wolf found a human voice. "Where you going?" it asked.

"I'll be back at midnight . . . with a stake that I'm gonna drive through your heart."

"Make it with onions," said the wolf. "Aaaggghh!" He went on writhing on the rug of the rented room as Hermie left to go look for a quieter place to study.

There was no one in the library. There were wheezes and creaks from the shelves that kept Hermie looking surreptitiously around. He felt a draft down the back of his neck and turned to see if the door was open. He changed his seat so that he was facing the door, then realized he was backed by the uncurtained windows that looked out, in the cool light of day, on the green. In the dark of night, however, the outside looked in at the solitary boy trying to study in the creepy library. There was a pre-fall windstorm moaning into strength outside, and the shapes of the trees blowing across the lights in the quad sent long-fingered shadows dancing around the library shelves.

Hermie knew there was no reason for him to be spooked. He'd spent too many evenings listening to "Inner Sanctum" and "Lights Out" . . . that was his problem. He shrugged his shoulders and tried to concentrate. It was all in the wind. He'd almost convinced himself and was settling into his studying when a door banged somewhere down the corridor. Hermie grabbed up his books and ran like hell . . . back to his cozy room, Oscy or no Oscy.

13

In the morning, after his second class, Hermie set out to look for the office of the college newspaper. He'd been putting it off because he'd been having second thoughts about trying out for it. He wasn't really that good a writer. His only experience'd been one poem in the high school yearbook, and a couple of letters to *Photoplay*. But those had been when he was a callow youth, so they didn't really count. It was a funny thing about confidence. In the quiet of your own room you were just loaded with it. You could see yourself ruling the world. But out in the big world, faced with all that competition, it was an entirely different matter. There was absolutely no reason in the world why Hermie Green should think he would make an adequate reporter for the college newspaper, but by the same token there was most likely no reason in the world why anyone else should either. Some people were so convinced about themselves, though, that they could convince you too. Sometimes it turned out that they were as good as they said they were. Sometimes they were nothing at all, just hot air. Actually, all the Editor could do was say no, so he had nothing to lose. Oscy had told him he could make it. "You use words no one ever heard of before. That should be in your favor."

The corridors and pathways were crowded with students in knots of twos or threes, going from one class to another, or just passing time aimlessly between lectures. Hermie, as usual, was alone and also, as usual, seemed to be going in the opposite direction from everybody else. He hoped that wasn't significant. In his super-sensitive mood everything seemed to hold some symbolic meaning for him. He found the building he was looking for and went in. The door was labelled "THE NUTMEGGER"— 'U. CONN'S OFFICIAL WEEKLY NEWSPAPER." He knocked, but nobody answered, so he walked on in.

The room he entered was a square room, small, with an old vinyl couch, some copies of last week's *Nutmegger* on a square coffee table and a door, half-open, that obviously led into the inner office. There was a boy sitting on the uncomfortable vinyl couch. He had the sickly expression of an applicant. Hermie recognized it. There was a ruckus of some kind going on in the inner office and the boy was trying not to listen. Hermie half-smiled at him and joined him on the couch. They both sat there, straining not to hear, but both totally fascinated by the argument that could be heard through the slit in the door.

". . . nor is this what I had been led to believe was the situation at the University of Connecticut." Girl's voice. Correction: *Pretty* girl's voice.

"Now look." Man's voice, or heavy-set, bespectacled boy's voice. Probably the Editor.

"No, I will not." Pretty girl again. "You have a parochial point of view and I don't intend to be poisoned by it. Obviously, three years as Editor of this eighteenth century publication has cause you to stand still while the world is passing by." Hermie was right. The heavy voice *was* the Editor.

"If you want my opinion . . ." Not-very-sure-of-itself-assistant-editor-type voice. Probably pimply.

"Well, that's about the *last* thing in the world I want." Hermie wondered what would be the *first* thing in the world she'd want. He had an intense desire to shower her with it, whatever it was. He knew she wouldn't want Pimply's opinion. She started up again and Hermie strained, not to miss a beat. "I'd rather leave it up to someone more impartial."

Before Hermie could collect himself, the Pretty Girl appeared in the doorway. Hermie was glad he'd been so accurate in his judgment. It was a good omen. Very Pretty Girl looked at the two boys sitting on the couch, then pointed to Hermie.

"I'll ask *this* man. You, sir . . . what is your name?"

Hermie remembered, thank God. "Hermie."

"Would you be good enough to step into this office, please? Did you say Hermie?" She reacted to the name, then tried to connect it to the face.

"Herman."

"Herman? As in Goering?"

Hermie knew this game. "As in Melville."

Pretty Girl seemed delighted. "Ah, good, a literary namesake." She didn't introduce herself. "Please come in. Won't take a moment." She held the door open for Hermie to walk through. Hermie walked in and faced Bespectacled Voice and Pimply. Right on all counts. Three out of three. He congratulated himself on his perception. Maybe he'd make a good newspaper man after all. Pretty Girl introduced him. "This gentleman, an expert on the works of Melville, is making himself available for an unbiased opinion." She seemed to be enjoying herself, and Hermie didn't think any of this was of any great moment to her.

"Listen," said the Editor. He *had* to be the Editor. He

was obviously born to be the Editor of a college newspaper. He wouldn't have fitted anywhere else. "Listen,
it's not necessary. Your story is lousy. So let's just . . ."

"He'll be the judge of that." The girl pointed to Hermie.
Right?" Then she answered for him. "Right." She picked
up a paper from the desk, and assuming a dramatic pose,
faced Hermie. "Now, listen to this opening paragraph and
tell me what you think of it. Take your time. Consider
the importance of your answer. Ready? Begin." She began
to read from the typewritten sheet of paper. "Last evening a fire raged in Larrabee Hall of unknown origin. It
is without doubt the work of an arsonist, evidently perpe-
trated in a fit of pique by a maniac with a match. Campus
officials, in an effort to pour cold water on the incident,
are immaturely calling it a case of spontaneous inflam-
mation, to which this reporter says 'Hah.' And this
morning, *you,* the student body, must face the fact that
somewhere on campus, there is among you . . . a man
with a match. Fire in Larrabee Hall. Shame on Connecticut U." She turned to Hermie with a flourish. "There."

"Right," said Hermie.

"What right?" asked the girl,

"Whatever you say right."

The girl pointed accusingly at the Editor. "Well, this
man here, this paragon of literature . . . he claims that
what I've written is sensationalistic, unclear and not
grammatical."

Hermie smiled. "Well, he's not altogether wrong."

The girl turned back to the Editor, as though Hermie's
point was in her favor. "See that, he agrees with you."
Everybody looked at her as if she were crazy. She turned
back to Hermie. "I want to thank you for your help.
You've found a home at this crummy rag, Herr Goering."
She gave Hermie a "Heil Hitler" salute. "*Auf Wiedersehen.*" Then she marched out, tossing her long hair for
emphasis.

The Editor, Pimply and Hermie stood looking at each

other in amazement, not quite sure what non-recurring phenomenon had just passed through their lives. The Editor recovered first and walked heavily into the waiting room. He asked the boy sitting there if he could do anything for him. The boy, permanently stunted in his growth by the events of the last few minutes, just shook his head in a silent no and bowed out backwards, not daring to run until he'd reached the safety of the corridor outside. Hermie watched him go. The boy, anxious to get out of the unwelcome limelight, ducked into a room, and just as quickly ducked out again when he discovered it was a girls' washroom. Hermie laughed with the others and they turned back into the office.

"Well, then," asked the Editor, "can I help *you?*"

"I don't know," Hermie said carefully. "I've written in high school. I thought maybe I could catch on here . . . as some kind of reporter."

"Well, it just so happens we have a recent vacancy. We'll try you. Here, fill this out."

As Hermie filled out the form, the Editor berated Pimply from out of the corner of his mouth. "No more Ace Girl Reporters."

"She wasn't my idea," Pimply protested.

"Well, she wasn't mine. Come to think of it," he scratched his head, "whose idea was she?"

"Hers," said Pimply.

"No more Ace Girl Reporters," repeated the Editor. This time he carved it in stone. Hermie smiled, but didn't look up from the form he was filling out.

14

Hermie wasn't very athletic, but he felt he had to go out for something. It was part of the college experience, going out for something. Also, Oscy said, it gave you a bit of headway when it came to girls. If you could wear a major letter it was worth almost as much as being good-looking, or rich.

Hermie didn't think he'd ever be a letter-man, but he did need some kind of exercise, and everybody said Track was probably the easiest. You didn't get banged around too much and you could pretty well choose your poison. It wasn't as glamorous as football, but you couldn't have everything.

He found himself out on the football field on a chilly October evening, standing around with a bunch of locker-room types, none of whom he'd ever noticed anywhere else on campus. They probably just came out when they smelled sweatsuits. The track coach, a burly Clark Gable with hairy ears, was engaged in some kind of silent colloquy with a clipboard. Hermie looked at the boys around him. If you judged by appearance, most of them looked athletic. He probably wouldn't even make the team.

Oscy had been the final persuader. "Listen, buddy, you've got endurance, and that cruddy conscience that won't let you off the hook. Anyway, let's face it, the four-minute mile is just a state-of-mind."

So there he was, shivering in shorts and an undershirt, feeling very self-conscious.

The coach finally closed the deal with his clipboard and joined the group. "Okay, fellas. I'm not interested in your names, just your performance. If you can run, we'll get along. Long distance men here, milers and half-milers here, dash men over there. Hermie plumped for the mile, figuring any less required a sprinter and any more required a fool.

After dividing them, the coach then brought them all together again and set them up in lines of six. "Tell ya what we're gonna do . . . when I give the signal, just run, as fast as you can. Stop only when you hafta. Got it?"

It seemed like an odd way to sort out the good from the bad. "What's Conn's record?" Hermie asked the ape next to him in line.

"We don't have one. We haven't made it to the Eastern Finals for fifteen years."

"Great," thought Hermie. "Nothing like joining up with a winning team."

Some of the boys were doing elaborate setting-up exercises on the football field. Bending, stretching, all that. One boy was on his thousandth, by count, jumping jack. One of the most efficient-looking athletes was deeply involved in very complicated leg-stretching exercises. Just before it came his turn to run, though, he pulled his right hamstring and wasn't able to compete. Hermie, not having worked out a series of setting-up calisthenics, ran in place for a couple of minutes and touched his toes ten times.

When the signal came for Hermie's line to run, he

started out with gusto, carelessly losing it on the first turn. By the second lap he had aged twenty years and slowed down to a dignified gentleman's trot. Going into the turn for the third lap he began to see red, white and blue stars in front of his eyes. Coming into the straight he gave up the ghost, or the ghost gave up him. It was a toss-up as to which of them made the decision. As he lay on the cinder track, breathing his last few breaths before renouncing this harsh cruel world forever, the coach passed by to check on whether he was alive or dead. With a burly foot that was probably as hairy as his ears, he kicked Hermie gently in the ribs.

"You all right?" he asked.

Hermie coughed in answer.

"You ever run before?"

"For Class President," Hermie gasped.

"Yeah, well, I hope we won't need you. But you never know. Sign your name on the board as you leave. Thank you for coming out."

"Thanks for the memory," mumbled Hermie.

He wrote up his experience much later for *The Nutmegger*. It was a very funny story. The Editor loved stories that put down muscles, probably because he didn't have any. Herm was very proud of it, his first story in print. He titled it "All experience is an arch, to build upon," a quotation of Henry Brooks Adams he'd found in an old yearbook.

15

Hermie sat in a drama class, but he wasn't really listening. First of all, the professor was one of those who was madly in love with his own voice and couldn't bear the sound of anyone else's. Second, Hermie had read all this stuff the night before. Thirdly, he had something else on his mind. He wasn't yet prepared to admit what it was that was on his mind. But it had long dark hair and a very fresh complexion, which ruled out the track coach. It also bounced when it walked and had an antic sense of humor, which eliminated Mrs. Gilhuly and Oscy.

Hermie had a quest. He was wondering how one went about tracking down something like that. Oscy was the expert but this wasn't the kind of thing he wanted to share with Oscy. To Oscy, girls were just glorified orifices, and this girl was different . . . oh, so different.

"And so we see clearly," the professor droned on, "how, in all of his plays, Eugene O'Neill wrote on two levels. *One* to entertain his audiences and . . . two, to do honor to Freud. . . . Why do I say that?"

A hand shot up. You haven't got a chance, thought Hermie. He wants to tell you the answer himself. Besides, it's in his lecture notes and he might lose his place.

The professor had an irritating throat condition and was constantly sucking on peppermints. Some of the boys insisted he was an alcoholic, and the peppermints disguised the fumes, but Hermie preferred to believe it was more innocent than that. When most of his ex-students heard the names O'Neill or Shaw, or Shakespeare, they always connected them to the overpowering smell of Professor Ford's mints. He felt around in his pockets, looking for a peppermint to ease his fevered throat. Hermie watched with half an eye as he followed his own train of thought.

How could he find out what her name was? He supposed he could ask The Editor or Pimply, but he wasn't ready to reveal himself yet, and he certainly didn't want to become one of those blind items at the end of the Editor's "Connversation Column." "What Freshman reporter is in pursuit of what pretty Frosh with a nose out of joint?" Maybe he could put an ad in the paper: Will the girl who lost the job on the *Nutmegger* last week please call the following number, where she will hear something to her advantage. No, that wouldn't do.

"I'll tell you why," the professor revealed, having located his peppermints. "Because O'Neill was a student of both drama *and* Freud. Are there examples?"

A hand shot up and was ignored as the previous one had been. . . . If she was interested in newspaper reporting, then she was probably an English major, which cut down the search somewhat. There were only about a thousand freshman English majors. He could rent a billboard. He'd always admired the Grand Gesture . . . the King of England giving up his throne, Romeo killing himself for love . . . but it probably cost too much. The billboard. Besides, what would he put on it? "Pretty Girl from the Editor's Office—I love you!" That wasn't quite him.

"Yes, take O'Neill's play "The Emperor Jones" written on two levels. What is the first level?"

Maybe drama. Maybe he should go along to a Drama Club rehearsal and see if she was there. That would be logical. She was pretty, and spirited. Perhaps he'd try that, if he could find out when the next rehearsal was.

"Action. Action showed Jones in flight from the natives whom he duped. And how did he dupe them? I'll tell you how."

Hermie tried to listen to the rest of the lecture, but on the pad in front of him he was doodling coeds with long hair and gorgeous smiles, nothing that O'Neill had ever felt important enough to concentrate on. Maybe she wouldn't be interested in him and the whole pursuit would be in vain. After all, he hadn't supported her against The Editor, and she'd called him Herr Goering. But then girls were supposed to admire men who wouldn't compromise their ideals. That was a touchy issue, though, because obviously she thought her reporting was first-rate, and obviously Hermie hadn't, so ideals didn't really enter into it. Just pride. Or vanity.

Hermie wasn't like Oscar, turned into a ravening wolf by anything that wore bobby sox and a pleated skirt. So he didn't entirely understand why he was put off his pablum by *this* girl. He tried to tell himself that he didn't want to make out with her, or anything like that. He just wanted to get to know her. That was it, increase his sphere of acquaintance. "Miss . . . whatever your name is, I'd like you to enter my sphere of acquaintance." No, that sounded phony, like something Oscy would pull on a dud in the soda shop. If someone like Cary Grant said that, it'd be debonaire and acceptable. On Hermie it sounded ridiculous. He decided to drop "sphere of acquaintance." It was too hard to fit into a sentence. Maybe "I'd like to know you better, Miss . . ." That was okay, but she might take it wrong or in the Biblical sense. She might think he was making a pass at her. Was he making a pass? Not really. He wasn't a pass-maker.

There should be a course in college. Hermie'd probably be the only one who'd sign up for it. None of the other guys seemed to have the same problems. Wherever he looked, people were in couples. They might have been getting ready to board the goddamned ark, they were so tightly coupled up. He could write a letter. But he didn't know her name. 'To whom it may concern . . .' sounded a bit impersonal. Anyway, he didn't know where she lived, either.

It bothered Hermie that when he should have been concentrating on O'Neill and Freud, or the War Effort, or calculus, or at the very least, whether or not to join a fraternity, he was worrying, like some kind of crazy, about how to get to know a girl whom he'd insulted the first and last time they'd met. He could try every sorority in college. They probably had lists, and she looked like sorority, but that wouldn't help because he still didn't know her name.

Hermie wandered out of his lit class and found himself in the Campus Coffee Shop. It must have been lunch time. He ordered a hamburger and a coke, and was eating it distractedly, paying perfunctory attention to a text beside his plate, trying to block out a particularly loud rendering of "Mairzy Doats" from the jukebox, when suddenly he realized he was being stared at. He looked up and My God It Was Her! . . . She . . . Her. He couldn't think straight. Miss . . . the girl from the newspaper office, sitting directly opposite him, at his table, at his gold-and-diamond-studded table, when he'd been half way around the world in his quest. There was a halo of light rays shooting out from behind her beautiful blonde hair. The music swelled in glorious crescendo as angel choirs rose to heaven, singing her praises. In slow motion he felt the last bite of his hamburger descending to stick in his gullet. The glass in his hand floated down to the table. The coke, as it spilled, swept in a graceful parabola over his *European History from the Middle Ages,* and spread in a slow-moving river over the face of Francis the First. Hermie shook his head to clear it, of the hamburger, and of the vision. He'd had these things happen to him before and he wasn't about to make a fool of himself this time. He found his tongue, surprisingly enough, just where it was supposed to be, and immediately made a fool of himself. "It's 'Mairzy Doats.' You see, I guessed that when they played 'Mairzy Doats' you'd be . . . I mean, where did you come from and what are you doing here . . . that is I was just studying my hamburger and having a bite of . . . my name's Hermie. . . ."

She ignored his nonsense and started talking as if she'd been there for an hour. She was perfectly at ease. "I know I have no flair for writing; none whatsoever. Still, I thought I'd give it a whirl." She picked up his doughnut and raised her eyebrows to ask if she could try it. "May I? Perhaps it's poisoned and you ought to know about it." Hermie nodded, still not quite believing. "Thank you." She took a bite and didn't get sugar all over her face like Hermie always did. "It's not poisoned. At least I haven't keeled over yet. And why you saw fit to agree with the criticism of those two midget minds will always be a mystery to me."

She didn't like him. He knew it. Hermie found his voice. "You asked for my opinion."

"I thought you'd lie."

"Why?"

"I hoped you'd like me enough." She did like him. "I could've picked the other boy, you know. You got the job of course."

"Sort of. I'm on probation. I have to submit a story on something in a week."

"How about the big fire in Larrabee Hall?"

"It's kind of . . . been done."

"Okay. But you'll see. When that story breaks, heads will roll."

Hermie nodded, not agreeing or disagreeing, but wanting to be pleasant so she'd stay around. Now that he saw her again in the flesh, she was even prettier than in his imagination. It was true, he now discovered, his fantasies didn't lie. He didn't know how to talk to girls.

She eyed him speculatively. "You fraternity?"

"No." She didn't like him, he could tell.

"You going to be?"

"I don't know." Jesus, he had to do better than this or the whole thing'd disappear into a dream again. "Do you come here often?" he asked in desperation.

"Only in the mating season," she answered. She was much better at this kind of thing than he was. He stole a glance around the coffee shop. Everyone was talking. Everybody had something to say. Some people had so much to say they couldn't even wait for the other person to finish before they broke in. Hermie wished he knew what in hell they were all batting about.

The girl didn't seem put off by his monosyllables. "It's important that you pick the right one."

Hermie'd forgotten what she'd been talking about. "Right what?" he asked brightly.

"Fraternity. I can help you. Give me a call." She liked him. She gathered up her books, and with a swish of her skirt was almost out the door.

God, he still didn't know her name! Hermie jumped up, overturning the rest of his coke, completely obscuring three hundred years of European History for ever. He ran after her. "Where do I . . . where can I call you?"

"At the sorority house," she said gaily.

"Which one?" Hermie could hear his voice rising in something close to hysteria.

She shook her head, smiling at his obtuseness. "Really, Hermie . . . is there another?" She paused. Hermie still looked dumbstruck. "Gamma Upsilon." She started walking away.

Hermie heaved a sigh of relief and started back to his table, then suddenly clapped his hand to his head. Christ! Hermie, you're a goddamned idiot! He chased her out into the corridor. "Your name . . . who do I ask for?"

"Ask for Julie." She walked away, then turned and waved. "*Auf Wiedersehen.*"

Hermie sat back in his chair, exhausted. Julie, of course Julie. She couldn't be anything else but a Julie. The unfortunate part of it was that Julies usually weren't for Hermies. Julies were for Jims and Ricks and Tonys. Hermies got Ritas or Gertrudes.

He watched her through the window as she hit the street. She seemed to know everyone, and more important, seemed to know what to say to make them laugh, or smile, or just wave as she passed by. She was his fantasy come to life, the girl he'd chased over half the boroughs of New York City and never found, the free-thinking, clean-limbed college girl of the Peck & Peck ads, with no pimples, no mother. A girl who wouldn't send you home on a cold subway train with blue balls.

Hermie was afraid he'd made an ass of himself. Julie was everything he wasn't. He wondered how long he could wait before calling her. He wrote down "Gamma Upsilon" before he forgot it. He didn't have to write down "Julie." He wouldn't forget that.

16

Mrs. Gilhuly handed Hermie a letter from home and a thin V-mail, from Benjie, when he came home that evening. He was dying to open it, but thought he'd wait until he and Oscy could read it together.

He was studying his still-damp "European History" when Oscy crashed into the room later that evening and plopped down onto his bed with a sigh. Hermie didn't bother to look up. He decided to do as much as possible before Oscy got through to his consciousness, which always happened sooner or later.

Oscy crossed his arms under his head and stared at the ceiling. "I have no interest in this college shit. As a result, my grades are headed for a new low. I will finish with a torrid F-minus. Hello, Hermie."

"I don't think there is such a thing," Hermie said automatically, not looking up from his book.

"They will invent it with me," said Oscy.

"You know what I think? It's a death wish. You *want* to flunk out."

"True. And, since I promised my old man I'd stay in school, I decided I'd give my athletic prowess a whirl." He stood up and went over to his bureau, where he found a tired-looking athletic supporter. He swung it around his head like Roy Rogers swinging a lariat. "And so, girding my powerful loins, and donning an iron jock . . . I tried out for the football team . . . and . . . I made it."

"What position?"

"Mostly Left Out."

"I didn't know that was a position."

"Hermie, you slay me. Left Out Behind the End . . . Left Out . . . Left Out . . . get it? Get it?" Oscy flipped the jockstrap over the bare light bulb that hung from the ceiling.

"Oh, yeah, I get it. Hah."

"Actually I can have any position I want. I could be coach if I want. My mother could be All-American here. Hermie, we have a tailback, Jack Scroggins, I believe he's blind. He can throw the ball a fuckin' mile, but he can't see past the line of scrimmage. It's a freak show. So the coach asks me to be the blocking back. What I do is drop back to protect Scroggins and while I'm doing that I scan the field for possible receivers. And when I spot one I shout to Scroggins where to throw the ball . . . like . . . "short to the right," and "deep down the middle." It's like Edgar Bergen and Charlie McCarthy."

"Does it work?"

"In practice it works to perfection." Oscy yawned and looked over at Hermie's books. "All that studying. You're gonna discover radium sure as shit."

"This is history."

"Well, it's all wet as far as I'm concerned."

Hermie turned the pages of his coke-dampened history book. "I'm afraid I have to agree with you for once." He closed the book and pushed it away. "We got a letter from Benjie. It's from 'somewhere in the Pacific.'"

"What's he say?"

"I thought we'd read it later."

"He's gonna get killed. You know that, don't you?"

"It's occurred to me," Hermie said.

"So I don't want to talk about it any more." Oscy flopped back on his bed.

"Okay." Good old Oscy. Don't talk about it and it'll go away. Maybe he was right after all.

Oscy had something else on his mind. "Look, Hermie, I know we agreed not to discuss our sex lives, but . . . I need some advice."

"In-Like-Flynn needs advice?"

"Okay, okay. I'm asking, aren't I? Where to begin. As you know, I don't do well with intelligent broads. Never did. It's never bothered me, because I think there's an indirect relationship between the size of the brain and the size of the boobs. So I'm not even trying with any of these Betty coeds. What I'm doing is scoring heavily with a real dummy . . . but with tremendous boobs."

"She's not in school?"

"I don't think she ever finished grade school."

"What does she do?"

"Everything." Oscy breathed out hotly and shook his hand loosely from the wrist.

"I mean where does she work?"

"She doesn't. I think she escaped from an asylum."

Hermie was sick of the conversation. He pulled his history book toward him again. "Look, forget it! Okay! Forget it!"

"Hermie, stay calm. It's a problem. All I know about her is that she picks me up in her car at 4 p.m., drives me to a garage . . . and rapes me. It's all very charming, but I'm not sure how long I'm gonna be able to go on with these rendezvous after a hard day of blocking for old Blind-Ass Scroggins."

"I feel for you, Oscar, I really do."

"Hermie, I wouldn't tell you this if it wasn't important to me. I need your expert advice."

"Why'nt you have her indicted for Statutory Rape?"

"Hah."

"Oscy, you're talking to the wrong person, but anyway, where'd you meet her?"

"In the bakery. I was getting horny and aggressive."

"Totally unlike your everyday self," Hermie said.

"As I said," Oscy repeated, fixing Hermie with a glare, "I was feeling horny and aggressive and I pointed out, as graciously as I could, that I thought she had a wild pair of cupcakes. Next thing I knew we were off to the races. . . . Her name is Glenda and . . . she helps me forget."

"I don't quite see where there's a problem."

"I'm not the man I used to be, Hermie. Being knocked on my ass all day on the football field, and then having to fill the breach every night. . . ."

"Why don't you form a back-up crew?"

"Hermie, you have no feelings." Oscy sighed and flopped over onto his stomach.

"Jesus, Oscy, what's happening to you?"

"I don't know. Maybe it's Change-of-Life. I'm gonna take a shower. A long shower. I may never come out. I'm feeling very low."

"Come on, let's go get a beer."

Oscy assumed the mantle of the martyr. He shook his head. "No, I don't want to disturb your studying."

"I'm through studying."

Oscy hadn't played out his scene fully yet. "Then I don't want to disturb your newspaper writing."

"I'm through writing."

"Then don't mind me. Go to sleep." Oscy's voice had descended to sepulchral. His self-pity was reaching its peak.

"I don't want to go to sleep."

Oscy suddenly cheered up. His depression gone, he threw open the closet door, dragged out his jacket, threw it over his shoulder and said, "Then why don't we go get a beer?"

"Jesus Christ!" said Hermie, tossing his papers in the air and sitting speechless at his desk while they floated back down, fanning out over the desk and floor in an intellectual snowstorm.

The boys found a bar that bore the reputation of not being too harsh on college boys. They both ordered beer. By the time the froth had subsided on Hermie's, Oscy was on to his second, and pretty soon, third glass. Because he wanted to get drunk, he wasn't finding it too easy. He was only slightly light-headed. Hermie sipped easily on his first beer. Oscy was reading Benjie's V-mail.

"The little rat—he's a Private First Class. How do you like that? And where do you suppose he is?"

"Beats me."

"Know what I think?"

"No one knows what you think," said Hermie.

"I think . . . I'll bet he's using our old code. You know, the lemon juice?"

"Why should he do that?"

"To tell us where he is. It's probably all here in lemon juice and he's waiting for us to figure it out. I need a match." He reached over and took one from the center of the table and struck it, Bogart-style, on the striker.

Hermie felt that Oscy was drawing attention to them and tried to stop him. "If he's not supposed to reveal what Theatre of Operations he's in . . . why would he go against the rules?"

"Because," said Oscy, bringing the match up to Hermie's face, "he's not a little goody two shoes like you." Hermie's face glowed in the glare of the match. "Ver ist der secret planss?" asked Oberlieutenant Hermlishhausen. "Torture me, pull out my finger nails, I'll never betray my country!" "Ver ist hidden deine President?" "Flay me, skin me alive, crush my balls, I'll never reveal that secret!" "Ver ist headed der Siebenth Army?" "Poke out my eyes, pull out my hair, that secret will die with me!" "Are you a goody two shoes?" "I cannot tell a lie. Yes, I am a goody two shoes." "Aha, ve haff discovered your secret. You vill die, Americanisher!"

Oscy had a couple more gulps of beer. The match was still alight in his fingers. "We'll soon see," he said. He held the match a distance from the letter, but the V-mail, tissue-thin, fanned by a draft, suddenly caught the flame and was alight. "Jesus!" He tried to fan out the flames without avail. He only succeeded in increasing them. Hermie picked up Oscy's beer and poured it over the burning letter. The flames were drowned, but the letter was burnt to a crisp. "Goddamned V-mail tissue paper! What the hell did you pour the beer on it for, Hermie?"

"To put out the goddamn fire, Oscy. Okay?"

"Not okay. Why didn't you use your goddamned beer?"

"I grabbed the nearest one."

"Why didn't you just piss on it?"

"Because it wasn't handy!"

Oscy crumpled the ashes of the V-mail letter in his hand and tossed them into the ash-tray. "Now we'll never know," he said sadly.

Hermie was getting impatient with his friend's odd mood. He felt he had enough problems of his own without taking on Oscar's seemingly manufactured ones. "What the hell is wrong with you, Oscy?"

Oscy was suddenly very depressed. He sunk his head into his arms, pushing his beer mug away. "I don't know. Maybe I'm pregnant."

"Come on," said Hermie. "Let's get out of here."

"Yeah," agreed Oscy, "Loose lips sink ships." He wobbled to his feet and Hermie led him gently out of the bar. Once on the street, Hermie let go of his arm. Oscy stumbled dramatically and fell to his knees.

"Go on without me," he told Hermie, in a trembling but brave voice. "Save yourself."

"No, old friend. If you go, we both go," Hermie said.

"I'm just a burden to you. Go back, comfort my wife, my children. She always loved you best."

"I could never face them if I left you here to die. I could never face myself again."

"Here, take the secret papers, deliver them to head-quarters." Oscy stretched out flat on the sidewalk, face down. It was getting cold and Hermie tried to pull him to his feet. The beer had finally gotten to him.

"Oscy, the M.P.s. They're heading our way. To your feet, man, quick."

Oscy reacted as Hermie hoped he would and stumbled to his feet. He still wasn't making much sense.

"Come on, Oscy, pull yourself together." Hermie pulled on Oscy's right arm, which threatened to leave its socket before Oscy began to move in the right direction.

"I am together, Herman, for the first time in my life I'm truly together. Tell me, where did I go wrong?"

Hermie tried to pull him back to reality. He thought they might get home quicker that way. "Well," said Hermie, "For one thing, what made you think Benjie was carrying around a lemon in his knapsack?"

"And why didn't you bring up that theory *before* I set fire to his letter?"

"Because I didn't think it would stop you."

"Hmmm. You're probably right." Oscy started nodding his head and was unable to stop, like one of those wooden birds that dips its head into water and is propelled by its own momentum to keep on dipping. "You certainly are a crafty devil, Hermie. You'll go far. Very far."

"Yeah, yeah," said Hermie. "Thanks for the vote of confidence, but let's get you home before Gilhuly sends out the constables."

Oscy was still nodding as Hermie half-dragged, half-carried him along the sidewalk. "The Pride of Erasmus

Hall, Little Goody Two Shoes. I don't know why I put up with you. . . ."

"Maybe because I'm your sole support at the moment." Hermie groaned, almost doubled up under Oscy's weight.

"You give me a complex, Goody."

"All right, Oscy, that'll do."

Suddenly Oscy had a new thought. "Know what I think?"

Hermie shook his head as best he could.

"I think we should send Benjie a couple of lemons. Maybe six."

"Right," said Hermie.

"Better yet, six pigeons. *Seven*. That'd surprise the shit out of the Japs, eh?" He began to sing, tunelessly, but loud. "Birds fly over the rainbow . . . why then oh why can't Benjie. . . ."

He sang the rest of the way home.

It was after ten and Mrs. Gilhuly never made an appearance. "Maybe she and the Baron really *do* have something going," thought Hermie.

17

Hermie figured Oscy's trouble was that he wasn't in the Army. It was a disease that was hitting a lot of their friends, and some of them had succumbed to it. Hermie had the same mixed feelings. By not going it was almost like putting all the weight of the war on a few slim shoulders. But could his going make all that difference? If his experience on the track team was any example, he was a rotten joiner, and would probably make a rotten soldier. Anyway, he really was enjoying college. He didn't think Oscy was. Oscy always liked to be where the action was, and he really hated to be standing by and not taking part. In fact, sometimes, if Oscy felt he wasn't in the middle of the action, he'd create his own action. He was well known in his section of Brooklyn as the founder of a good many spectacular ruckuses. Rucki?

Hermie had gone over and over the same thoughts so many times, yet he knew that whatever conclusion he reached in his head, he was much too compliant to do anything about it. Maybe a bit of a coward. Not a physical coward but a sort of moral coward. He'd be letting down his father and his mother and his sister and even his history teacher, if he suddenly changed his mind and joined up. He made a lot of excuses to himself as to why he had to stay behind. None of them were very reassuring in the middle of the night when he couldn't sleep. Then he made all kinds of romantic and daring decisions, saw himself waving goodbye, going straight to the front, becoming an instant hero, returning on a stretcher, being cheered by crowds as the President knelt to pin a medal on him. But when he looked at himself in the light of an average morning, he realized he knew himself pretty well, and whether he liked it or not, he wasn't about to make any dramatic moves. He had a dreaded feeling that Oscar didn't have many arguments left, though.

Hermie hadn't mentioned Julie to Oscy, and wasn't about to. One evening, when Oscy was away, probably impregnating Glenda, Hermie quietly crept to the pay phone in the hall at Mrs. Gilhuly's, hoping no one was around. He dialed and waited. A female voice answered. What did he expect, a male voice?

"Hello?" said Hermie." "Is this Gamma Upsilon?" At least that's what he intended to say. What actually came out was complete gibberish, understandable only to the most alert listener.

"I beg your pardon?" asked the polite female on the other end of the line.

He tried again. Of course it was Gamma Upsilon. He didn't have to reassure himself of that. He'd checked the number, hadn't he? Anyway, it was too hard to say when you were in the state Hermie was in. "May I please speak with Julie? This is . . . Hello?"

At least it had come out more clearly, but the girl had gone before he could say who he was. Suppose there was more than one Julie at Gamma Upsilon. It wasn't a terribly uncommon name. If he got some other girl on the end of the line he'd be completely speechless again. Maybe he wouldn't be able to tell. He couldn't remember just how she sounded. Sometimes all girls sounded alike on the phone. He waited and sweated, the receiver in danger of slipping right out of his damp hand. Perhaps the girl hadn't gone away. Perhaps they'd just been disconnected. "Hello?" he spoke into the receiver. Nothing. He jiggled the phone and instantly disconnected himself. Goddamned idiot! He ran like hell back to his room and got another nickel. He dialed carefully, afraid of forgetting the number.

The phone was quickly picked up at the sorority house. "Hello?" It was Her, he was sure.

He began to shake with nervousness. "Hello? Julie? Diss iss Herr Goering. . . . Who? Janie? No, I wanted to speak to Julie." He felt like a Royal Ass. Stupid Janie would probably go running to tell everyone about the lunatic who was calling Julie, and Julie wouldn't want anything to do with him, and that would be the end of that. There was an ominous silence on the end of the line. Then: "Hello?" *That* was Julie! How could he have made such an idiotic mistake. Now he remembered exactly how she sounded, and it was nothing like the other girl at all.

"Hello? Julie? Ach yes. Diss iss Herr Goering calling, from der Front. Yes. Yes, der Fuhrer gafe me your number undt I was thinking . . . how vould it be if you undt I choined forces on Saturday night?" There, it was out. Phew!

One of Mrs. Gilhuly's other boarders was waiting to use the phone and kept coming out of his room to see if Hermie was through. Hermie lowered his voice. "Oh, I see."

"I can't hear you," Julie said, on the other end.

"I said, 'Oh, I see'," Hermie yelled into the phone,

then, quieter, "Vell, den, how does Friday night strike you? . . . I said FRIDAY NIGHT!"

The boarder raised his eyebrows. Nobody'd ever heard Hermie yell before.

"Oh, sure . . . I understand. What? Oh, sure! How do I get there? Ah, you have a car. Okay, I'll be downstairs in one minute. Half-hour? Oh, sure. Okay." He started to hang up the phone, then suddenly realized she didn't know where he lived. He tried yelling into the mouthpiece, hoping to resurrect her, maybe she hadn't quite hung up. "Listen do you know where I live?" he hollered at the buzzing sound the phone was making in his ear. "Hello? Hello?" Nothing. She'd gone. Disconnected. Perhaps forever. Another great episode in the life of Hermie, the Hopeless Hermit.

"All right, already," said the impatient boarder. "Hang a candle in the window. If she can't find you they'll send out a St. Bernard with a keg of titty milk. Would you please be so kind as to relinquish the phone?" Hermie didn't realize he was still hanging onto it like a lifeline. "I have an important call to make to the War Department. Some Japanese ships have been sighted in the college swimming pool."

With a flash and a flamboyance that Hermie could only envy, the other boarder dialed a number and was instantly connected. "Hello? War Department? Hey, wanna fight, baby?"

Hermie went back into his room and looked at himself in the mirror. It wasn't the most promising of faces, but it wasn't that bad either. He wondered which looked better, the hair over his forehead, or brushed back. He tried it both ways but couldn't decide. He really needed a shave, but he thought maybe he looked at bit more mature when he had a five o'clock shadow. Actually he didn't usually get a five o'clock shadow until about ten o'clock the next morning, but that was strictly classified information, and certainly not for general distribution.

His clothes he couldn't do much about. All his white shirts were at the laundry. That would've been too formal anyway. It was a toss-up between the green-and-white checkered shirt with a missing button, or his college sweat shirt. There was no use looking through Oscy's stuff. Most of it was under the bed, and Oscy wasn't the last word in sartorial elegance anyway. Most of Oscy's shirts could stand up by themselves. Hermie wondered why any girl would have anything to do with Oscy. Maybe that's why Oscy had such a promiscuous love-life. Every girl he went with insisted he take off his clothes before she could come near him, and that was how it all began. Thinking about that, Hermie gave a fleeting thought to his own underwear, just in case. He wasn't wearing the pair with the run, was he? No, that was a couple of days ago. He blushed at his own presumption.

Going back to Oscy, he really couldn't understand why any girl would have anything to do with him. Then why would any girl want anything to do with Hermie? He would have to assume the only reason was that there was a desperate shortage of males at Conn, or maybe she had detected something special in Hermie. His brain, perhaps. But he hadn't shown her much evidence of that in the encounters they'd had so far. Maybe she just wanted to get back on the paper and was using him as a stepping stone. Or maybe she was just playing games with him and wouldn't show up. After all, she hadn't asked where he lived. How did she get gasoline stamps? Perhaps she was a foreign spy. He'd heard of stranger things. Well, she wouldn't get anything out of him. He gave the mirror his staunch patriot stare. No doubt about that face. It belonged to an American, through and through, tried and true, true blue to the last ditch. Yes, sirree! They could do what they would to him. He changed his expression to reflect his stiff-upper lip look. He thought he looked a bit like Sir Winston Churchill in that one.

What was he going to talk to this girl about? He hardly

knew her. Matter of fact, he couldn't even remember
what she looked like. He wouldn't recognize her when she
came to pick him up. He'd get in the wrong car and end
up with the Dean of Women. Maybe they'd have nothing
in common, he and Julie, that is, not the Dean of Women.
They might sit in silence for two hours, studying the table
in front of them and thinking of something to say. Hermie
had to admit to himself he wasn't the world's most con-
fident man.

He decided to think positive. He was, without a doubt,
the best looking man in this room. He had a superior
brain, or at least his mother had always told him so. He
had a vivid and exciting past. What woman wouldn't fall
for his charms? Julie, probably, that's who.

A sudden blast from a car horn in the street below
quickly ended Hermie's reverie. It was the sweatshirt and
an under-confident Hermie who descended the stairs to
meet Julie. He missed the last step, but made a quick
recovery, and only blushed slightly as he got into her car,
an old pre-War Ford, on the passenger side.

Suddenly he remembered what Julie looked like. How
could he have forgotten? How could he ever forget? She
looked sensational. It wasn't what she wore. Well, maybe
it was what she wore. She had on some sort of a lace
blouse that was open way down to her knees, or somewhere in that region. Not that Hermie dared look. On
top of it she had a blue sweater the exact color of her
eyes. Hermie didn't have to look directly at her to get
that. He could see her reflection in the rearview mirror
when he craned his neck just slightly. He thought she had
on blue jeans and saddle-shoes. But he couldn't have
sworn to it in a court of law.

They rode in silence for a while, Julie handling the
wheel very firmly and well. Finally she spoke. "I was
beginning to wonder if you were ever going to call. Matter
of fact, I was fully prepared to have you not call. So . . .
when you did call . . ."

"I was trying to get myself squared away. You know . . . adjusted."

"Yes, I guess each of us has to adjust to a new environment. I accept that. That makes sense. That's reasonable."

"I was going to call you earlier but I had some tests to study for."

"Ah, the exigencies of college life. It's a rude awakening after high school to realize how much is expected of us. Yes, it's eye-opening."

"I agree."

"When you're in high school you think college is going to be just a continuation of the same kind of thing, school and classes and social things. But it's not. It's very different. In college each person has to make his own life, his own schedules."

"Right."

"We're no longer wrapped up in the womb of home and school and family. It's the beginning of the real world and the most important thing is to learn how to manipulate it."

Hermie had a sudden flash that put him immediately at ease. Julie was just as nervous as he was. He wondered how many times she'd changed clothes before she left Gamma Upsilon. "Do you always talk so much? I mean non-stop?" he asked.

"Only when people keep looking at me. Do you always keep looking at people? I mean non-stop?"

Hermie smiled. "Only when they keep talking."

"Touché," laughed Julie.

"Ditto," said Hermie, relaxing. It wasn't so hard to talk after all.

"You've never really been away from home, have you?"

"Couple months at summer camp. I made belts and ashtrays and learned about trees. My folks came up every weekend. How'd you know?"

Julie shrugged. "I can tell. I'm glad about the trees, though. I like that. I heartily approve."

"This isn't your first time away from home."

"Oh, I've been to schools." There was a whole history in her answer.

"Your daddy's rich."

"Yeah, and my Ma is goodlooking." Julie said it bitterly. Hermie felt that she meant something else entirely. He felt a flush of warmth for her. You couldn't call it love because he hardly knew her. He wanted to wrap her up and look after her.

The sky seemed darker as they drove further out into the countryside. There were fewer street lights and only an occasional house. It was a very starry night. Hermie wasn't at all sure that all the stars were in the sky. He put his arm along the back of her seat, but didn't touch her. He knew she knew it was there. And she knew he knew she knew.

When they came to a quiet spot at the end of what seemed to be a dead-end lane, Hermie leaned over and very gently put his foot on top of Julie's, forcing her to brake to a stop. She turned off the ignition and Hermie tried to put his arms around her. She gently pushed him away and got out of the car. He climbed across the seat and followed her. It was quiet, the stillness of eternity, and an eternity before either of them spoke. Hermie backed her up against a tree and kissed her lightly on the forehead. She didn't resist, so he put his arms around her and began to press his body against hers. She broke free and pulled away, smiling at him, a little unsure of herself, he thought.

Hermie had an insight that helped him relax a bit. She wasn't as sure of herself as she seemed. There was a good deal of bluff there.

"This is a . . . sugar maple tree," Hermie said, examining it with the pursed lips of an expert, as she ducked under his arm.

"There's got to be another tree," Julie said.

"Yeah, definitely a sugar maple." He followed Julie and fell in step beside her, "Hi," he said.

"Hi," she answered, heading back to the car.

Hermie stopped her and held her by the arms. "Why'd you pick me?"

"What?"

"Why me?"

"Well, in case you haven't noticed . . . there aren't many men on campus."

"There's enough. And most of 'em are older than I am. You're probably older than I am."

"I was eighteen July 23rd."

"I was eighteen April 13th."

"Then your worries are over."

Hermie edged her up to another tree, and surrounding her gently, not using any force, he managed to get her into his arms. He leaned over and examined the tree. "I'd say . . . sycamore. This is a sycamore tree." He kissed her, catching her just where he wanted, right on the lips.

Julie stayed for a moment, then said quickly, "Big fire in Larrabee Hall," and ducked again, but this time he caught her. "I thought you'd be shy," she said.

"I am."

"Oh, sure."

"But where I come from, what we try to do is establish our masculinity right off."

"Consider it established. Now can we get to know each other?" She broke free, successfully this time, and headed back to the car.

Hermie re-examined the tree with a professional frown. "On second thought, it could be a slippery elm," he said to himself. He followed her back to the car, pleased with himself and with his performance. Julie had started the car already. She smiled shyly at him as he slid in.

"It's late, okay?"

"Okay," he said, letting his hand rest on her shoulder

this time. It was so easy once you stopped monitoring your own performance. They drove silently back to Hermie's rooming house, perfectly comfortable in their silence. Hermie had read somewhere that a real relationship was measured by its silences. If they were easy, then the relationship was okay. He smiled to himself.

"How did you know where I lived?" he asked.

"Radar," she said.

"No, really."

"It's easy, I asked your friend."

"Oscy?" He was flabbergasted. Oscy had actually kept a secret!

As he got out of the car, Julie leaned out of the window. "Now I want to ask *you* something, Hermie. Was that last tree really a sycamore?"

"I haven't the slightest idea," he said, touching his fingers to her lips, then to the tip of her nose. She drove away. Hermie felt that somewhere along the way the initiative had changed hands. She'd let him take it and he liked that.

He watched until she turned the corner. He'd forgotten to ask her when he could see her again. He ran in and stood by the phone, timing her trip home, her parking the car, her walking upstairs and, just as he thought she'd be passing the phone in the hall, he dialed.

She picked it up on the first ring. "Gamma Upsilon."

"Hi," said Hermie.

"How'd you know it was me?"

"Radar. Anyway, I have my spies all over. Don't try to evade The Shadow."

"I won't. I won't. But it's cold out here."

"I had a nice time, Julie."

"Me, too." She paused. "Good night, Hermie." She hung up the phone softly.

Mrs. Gilhuly tromped up the stairs and gave Hermie a look. "I hope that wasn't an incoming call," she said."

"No, that was definitely outgoing," Hermie answered, smiling. "Good night, Mrs. Gilhuly."

It wasn't until he was back in his room and half-ready for bed that he realized he still hadn't made another date.

Oscy was asleep when Hermie got in, which was a blessed relief. Hermie had no interest in sharing Julie with the wolf-man, even if he did know of her existence. Oscy had fallen asleep with a much-thumbed copy of *Forever Amber* on his face. Hermie gently removed it and was going to put it on Oscy's bureau when his eye caught a phrase. He started reading and wasn't able to put it down. He didn't believe people dared print stuff like that. It was dawn by the time he finally fell asleep.

18

It was Oscy's first League Game and Hermie was supposed to report on it for the *Nutmegger*. Julie was with him, wrapped in a school scarf and big fur mittens. What was happening down on the field didn't look too much like football. A bunch of guys hitting at each other with brilliant disorganization was more like it. Players seemed to topple over without reason. The ball was alive and elusive. A kicker tried a field goal and struck the hand of the holder, who rolled over and groaned in pain. The Marx brothers would have needed practice to improve on it. The Connecticut team wasn't even completely in uniform. One of the backs was wearing a green shirt. The rest were in gold and black. They all had different stripes on their socks. The Center was having trouble with his shoulder pads, which kept slipping until they looked more like sprouting wings. On the sideline the extra players were stretched out in various positions of repose. One was reading a newspaper, one was smoking a cigarette, cupped in his palm to hide it from the coach. The cheerleaders, having shouted themselves hoarse, to absolutely no avail, had retired defeated and could be seen spotted throughout the stands, with basketball players. One of them had covered the black and gold uniform, not sure that she even wanted to be connected with the team in any way.

Hermie was trying to write something for the paper about the game. He scratched an occasional note. Julie leaned over, looking at his pad, fascinated. "What are you writing? They're not *doing* anything."

"Ah," said Hermie, "It may look that way to you."

"Well, how does it look to you?"

Hermie looked up. "It looks like they're not doing anything."

Julie reached over and kissed him on the cheek. Hermie rubbed it off and looked around. "Shameless hussy! I'm on an assignment. Don't fool with an ace-reporter in pursuit of his story!"

Julie pretended submission. "Right, sir! Sorry, yer 'onor," she said, saluting. He put his arm around her furry coat and squeezed.

"My God, you've put on weight!" he said.

"It's the coat, silly. It's bearskin."

"Looks pretty well covered to me," Hermie flicked his eyebrows in a Groucho Marx imitation, then quickly turned his attention back to the field, where nothing was happening. "Let me work, woman."

The players were in a huddle on the forty-yard line. Scroggins was giving enough instructions to fill a notebook. The huddle broke and moved to the line of scrimmage. The whistle blew, someone was off-side, and they tried again. Again the whistle blew. Scroggins and Oscy moved back in Ye Olde Single Wing Attack. Scroggins was directly behind Oscy. He squinted his eyes almost shut as he called the signals, "25 - 38 - 47 - hut, hut, hut."

The ball came flying back to Scroggins, almost shooting

over his shoulder before he found it. He grabbed it and dropped back to pass, Oscy dropping back with him, his arms ready to block, his legs firmly planted astride the turf. Scroggins cocked his arm to throw as Oscy looked over the field. Forced to make a split-second decision, he found he couldn't. Players from the other team were beginning to pour through the offensive line. Oscy still hadn't a signal to give to Scroggins.

"Where? Where?" asked the almost-blind quarterback, urgently.

"Well," Oscy hesitated.

"Where?"

Oscy took a deep breath and plunged. "Deep and to the . . ."

Too late. Three men hit Scroggins and he was pounded into the turf, three feet deep.

". . . left," finished Oscy.

Somehow or other the ball squirted free of the squirming players on the ground. Oscy stood there and watched as two five-hundred pound monsters descended on him, all teeth and claws, first devoured him, then spat him out into the mud. He went down like a sack of loose shit, perhaps never to rise again.

A million whistles blew, but it was all over for Oscy. The other team gave a resounding cheer, probably as much for Oscy's aid to their defense as to the fact that they'd just won the game, 314 to zilch.

Up in the stands, Julie looked confused. "Hermie, something went wrong. Right?"

"Right," said Hermie, tearing up his notes and tossing the pieces into the air. "I guess my first article better be on bird calls."

He and Julie walked down to the field to get Oscy. Covered in mud and disgust, Oscy was scarcely fit company. They decided to take him for a hamburger to cheer him up. Hermie'd noticed that whenever Oscy was ahead of the game, any game, he didn't want to eat. When he fell behind he was always ravenous. He figured today for a six-hamburger day. He checked his pocket to make sure he had enough.

Oscy was trying to hide under a large checkered mackinaw, which looked odd over the football shoulder pads, and didn't do such a fantastic job of disguising him anyway. His face was streaked with mud and sweat.

He'd've preferred mud and glory, but his was not to reason why.

"It wasn't that bad, Oscy. You just didn't have good blocking," Hermie said.

"I think it was the cheerleaders. They gave up too easily," Julie said.

"No, I analyzed Oscy's game," Hermie said, "and I think he should have been playing at first base."

"That's baseball, sports-writer!" They were Oscy's first words.

"Thank God it talks," said Hermie, delighted to have raised at least a reproach.

"It's a bird!" said Julie.

"It's a plane!" said Hermie.

"It's Super-Oscar!" They all three yelled together.

"You know," said Hermie thoughtfully, "maybe I could get a job on the other team's newspaper."

"Actually," said Oscy, recovering enough to form intelligible words, "it's not as bad as it looks."

"It isn't?" Hermie asked.

"No, it's worse," said Oscy.

"Who do you play next?"

"The WACs. They're a two-touchdown favorite," Oscy said grimly.

"Seriously, Oscy . . . I'm trying to write a story."

"You better stick to fantasy."

"Oscar, you don't appreciate it right now, but this afternoon's game *was* pure fantasy. It never happened. It couldn't've. No team could play that badly and live."

"Who said I was living?"

"Are you hungry?"

"Starving."

"You're living. But seriously, Oscy, what am I going to write?"

"Hermie, you're a registered pain in the ass. You keep on saying 'But seriously Oscy'. Personally I don't give a shit what you write."

"Thanks. Spoken like a friend."

"All right. You want to write something? How about taking down my resignation."

"Come on, Oscy, you can't quit."

Oscy was still morose. "Smile when you say that. It's quit or die. Take this down. "I, number 49, being of sound mind and busted ass, do hereby request that my jersey be retired and that my remains be transferred to the Tiddly Winks Team."

"Let's go eat," said Julie, leading the way into Hamburger Heaven. "You'll feel better after you eat."

"I'll never feel better again," grumbled Oscy, but he followed them into the place anyway.

When they'd ordered, Julie turned to Oscy. "Tell me, old number 49 . . ."

"I wish you wouldn't call me by my ex-number. Call me by my new number. Number 2."

"Don't you have a girlfriend around here?"

Oscy glanced at Hermie to see if he could judge how much Julie knew. To Julie he shook his head. "No one to speak of."

Hermie had to defend himself, even though no one was attacking. "I didn't say anything."

Oscy was still glaring at Hermie.

"Look, I didn't tell *him* about *you*," Hermie appealed to Julie. "And I didn't tell *her* about . . . *her*." He turned back to Oscy. "Okay?"

Oscy wasn't totally convinced.

Julie didn't let it rest. "Who is 'her'?"

"An acquaintance." Oscy bit deep into his Number 4,

a cheeseburger with bacon, tomatoes and blue cheese, smothered in onions, and once Oscy got hold of it, ketchup, mustard and mayonnaise. His voice, of necessity, was muffled. In fact, it was a wonder he didn't die right there from the chemical shock of that combination in his stomach. Hermie could only assume that long years of abuse had fused the lining of Oscy's stomach into case-hardened steel. Sold to the war effort he'd probably yield a victory load of bullet casings.

Julie persisted. "Is she sorority?"

"Yeah," Oscy mumbled through a mouthful of french fries. "Alpha Bumper Humper."

Julie wisely ignored what was none of her business and went on with something else that was none of her business. "Listen, gang . . . how come you two aren't in a fraternity?"

"We're homos," growled Oscy.

"Well, you play *football* that way," said Julie.

Oscy laughed. He liked her. She wasn't his type but he liked her. "Touché, heh, Hermie?" He smiled at Hermie.

"Tell her, Oscy, tell her the fraternities you're interested in. Tell her the ones you mentioned. You know, the one with the rubber duck?"

Oscy side-stepped it nicely, and answered, pseudo-serious, "Yes. I believe it was . . . Alpha Rubber Duck."

Julie was serious. "The two of you are missing out. For one thing, that rooming house food has to be poison."

"We only have breakfast there."

"What about dinner?"

"We dine at various Salvation Army missions. We know most of the hymns," said Oscy.

"Okay." Julie could see she'd have to lay it out for them. "The trick is to get into the *right* fraternity."

"And which one is that?"

"The one I pick for you," she said, self-assuredly. She

knew she had them charmed. They weren't going to argue.

"And that's all there is to it?" asked Oscy.

"No. There's your initiation."

"What's that?" Oscy was suspicious.

"Well . . ." Julie hesitated for the first time. Hermie thought there was something ominous in that, but didn't discover what until much later. Oscy was well into his fifth hamburger and feeling much better. Anything Julie said was all right with him.

"Just get us the gen," said Oscy.

"What's gen?" asked Hermie.

"I don't know. I heard it in an English Air Force movie. It means information, I think."

"We'll find out next he's with the enemy," said Hermie.

"Then I'd say our side'd have a good chance of winning," laughed Julie. "I'll call you later, after I've got the 'gen'. Okay?"

"Okay." Hermie mouthed a silent kiss at her as she threaded her way through the tables.

"Nice girl," said Oscy.

"Thanks," said Hermie.

"Too good for you, though. Do you have enough money for an ice cream soda? I'm starving."

Hermie dreamed about Julie that night. She was dressed in something diaphanous, almost completely transparent. He was following her through some woods, it seemed, except every now and then there'd be a door that she'd skip through. Then he'd have to come up with the right password to get through to where she was. The minute he'd get through the door, he'd see her, already way ahead of him, but beckoning him on. She looked fantastic, absolutely edible, and Hermie was panting in his effort to catch up with her. Oscy appeared once from behind a tree, eating a hamburger and not at all interested in Julie. Hermie waved at him and tried to tell him to

stop Julie so he could catch her, but Oscy just waved his
hamburger and went back behind the tree. Finally, the
doors stopped and Hermie found himself in an enormous
room. There was a fancy dress ball going on. Everyone
was masked and he couldn't find Julie. He danced with
each woman in the room in a frantic effort to find her.
One woman had a gown made completely of pearls. The
pearls kept dropping off, just like the woman in *Forever
Amber,* until she was totally nude. Hermie couldn't have
cared less. He was getting more and more frantic in his
search for Julie. Suddenly he faced one last door. He
knew she was on the other side of it, but couldn't get up
the courage to open it. Somehow, it opened by itself and
Julie was indeed there, lying on a couch, holding out
her arms to him. He went toward her and woke up, his
bedsheet a bedouin tent over the protruberance that was
Hermie. He swore loudly, turned over on his stomach
and tried to go back to sleep.

He couldn't though. The dream had completely un-
nerved him. It wasn't as bad as the one he'd had a couple
of nights ago when, just as he'd been going to enter
Julie, she'd turned into Mrs. Gilhuly, but it was bad
enough. He went to get a glass of water and sneaked
Oscy's copy of *Forever Amber* from under his bed. It
was the hottest book he'd ever read that came in a regular
cover. He couldn't believe most of it. And a *woman* wrote
it! He entertained himself with that until he heard Mrs. G.
ringing the breakfast bell.

19

True to her word, Julie came to them the next day at lunch with the information. The fraternity was Pi Epsilon Tau, and they were starting pledging that very day.

"What do we have to do to join?" Oscy asked.

"Oh, they'll tell you what. I gave your names to a senior I know, so they're expecting you. Just be there tonight at seven."

"Oh, how unfortunate, I have a Tiddly Winks Championship at seven," said Oscy.

"You can miss it this once," said Hermie. "You'd better go or I'm not going."

"It'll be a breeze for you two. Look, I gotta go crack the books. Don't look so nervous. It'll be groovy as a movie."

"See you later, after the frat thing?" Hermie asked Julie.

"Mm, sorry, I gotta wash my hair. Bye, boys." She

breezed away, nodding and waving to different people in the lunch room.

"Hmm," said Hermie. "That wasn't like Julie."

"What wasn't?" asked Oscy.

"The language. She doesn't usually talk like a jive chick. There's more here than meets the eye."

"Ah, how bad could it be?" Oscy took off for a two o'clock. "See ya there at seven."

Oscy was the last to arrive, red-faced and panting, at the Pi Epsilon Tau house. Hermie was already there, along with eight other Pledges. None of the Pledges looked too sure of themselves. They were dressed in old clothes, and looked apprehensively at the senior members of the fraternity who were standing by with their paddles at the ready.

Oscy tried a "Heil Hitler" to the head guy and got in return a frown that went deeper than any disapproval Oscy'd ever felt before. It traveled right down to his toes and back up his spine. He thought a heart attack might feel something like that. He managed a sickly smile, all that was left of his usual super-confidence, and stepped back into line with the other Pledges. They were in such a state of open terror that not one had even thought of grinning at Oscy's intrepidity, let alone trying it out. Hermie felt sorry for Oscy, for probably the first time in his life. He gave him a thumbs-up sign from behind his back. He didn't know whether Oscy caught it or not, but at least the goodwill might help him through. The President introduced himself.

"I'm the President of Pi Epsilon Tau. This night marks the beginning of your initiation." His voice was like ice, but colder. Hermie thought he looked a bit like Attila the Hun in one of his angry moods. "This night also marks your separation from boyhood." Hermie was afraid it might also mark his separation from his spine. "Some of you will survive and go on to become true men

of Pi Epsilon Tau. Others of you will fall by the way-
side. . . ." Patton, commanding the Third Fucking Army
couldn't have been more devastating in his contempt at
the failure of one of his men to overcome an objective.
"If any among you have doubts as to his ability to withstand these tests of character, or if, for any reason, you
wish to drop out *now* . . . step forward. You have five
seconds."

Hermie sneaked a glance around. Every one of the
Pledges looked as if he would have been less afraid of
dropping dead than of dropping out now. Oscy had
recovered enough to get an 'I dare you' look on his face.
Hermie admired his temerity.

There was no response to the President's challenge.
"Then let the games begin," said Great Caesar.

Hermie experienced a momentary blackout. Suddenly
he remembered something that had terrified him one
wintry day in New York City. His mother had taken him
up to Manhattan to meet Cousin Sophie, who had an
hour to spend between trains on her way from Miami to
the west coast. The three of them, his mother, Sophie
and Herman, had been sitting in the Automat, catching up
on the marriages, deaths and babies in the family. At
least, his mother and Cousin Sophie had. Hermie was
much more interested in what went on behind the little
windows where the food was on display. He'd been doing
his damndest to catch a glimpse of someone behind the
panel, when his attention was diverted by the piercing
horn of an automobile outside in the street. Everyone in
the cafeteria had turned around, because the blast of the
horn kept on piercing the regular Manhattan noise for a
much longer time than was normal, even for an angry
cabbie. Trying to figure out where the noise was coming
from, Hermie finally realized that it came from a big
panel truck double-parked in front of the automat. A tall
boy in a college sweater was standing at the back of the
truck with a paddle in his hand, and herding out of it the

most horrendous group of 'things' Hermie'd ever seen.
Hermie felt his flesh crawl. He thought they must be
creatures from another planet. They were college-man
size and were totally naked except for a heavy layer of
oily looking mud all over their bodies. Their heads were
shaved, except for a strip across the top and down the
back, Mohawk-style. Hermie, big as he was, had practically jumped into his mother's lap in terror, screaming.
His mother, who feared for her life every time she lit the
gas stove, was no particular comfort. He could feel her
knees shaking. Cousin Sophie, who knew all about those
things, explained that the strange-looking boys were
Freshmen Pledges going through some kind of initiation
into a fraternity. They probably had to get back to the
frat house under their own steam. Hermie had nightmares
for weeks afterwards about Indians with tomahawks
chasing him through the streets of Manhattan.

He suddenly thought of that now, and was a shaking
lump of jelly as he had been then, ten, twelve years ago.
God, if they did something like that, he'd die!

Hermie felt a silence and realized they were waiting
for him. The President was eyeing him like Mussolini
might eye a reluctant soldier. One of the seniors had his
paddle raised. Hermie scuttled after the other Pledges
who were gathered in the short hallway of the frat house.
As Hermie entered the hallway, one of the seniors dragged
a road-mender's barricade and sealed the reluctant freshmen into an area roughly the size of a toilet booth. One
of the senior Pi Epsilon men took a container of eggs
from an enormous pile on the floor by the diningroom
door and handed it to one of the other seniors.

"I am the Flight Commander," he announced. There
was no doubt in any of the Pledge's minds that he was
exactly what he said he was. "Gentlemen, we have our
orders. It's a dangerous assignment and a great test of
your skill. Also, these bombs are expensive and hard to

come by. So . . . make every one count. Line up, choose
your payloads."

The seniors lined up and each picked up three or four
boxes of the eggs and climbed the stairs to the first landing. When they were all upstairs, the Flight Commander
looked at his watch. "All right, gentlemen, consider the
altitude and the wind velocity. There should be no flak,
although there is a full moon. Zero hour. Lead man . . .
go!"

The lead man took an egg from the container, held
it in his hand for a moment, bounced it speculatively on
his palm, squeezed it, then, sighting something below in
the hallway, held his egg over the railing, poised, waiting
for the signal, in perfect control of all his reflexes.

"Bombs away!" ordered the Flight Commander. At the
signal, the lead man delicately released his egg, which
splattered, right on target, on the head of Hermie, below.
The eggy goo slid from his head and oozed, in a sticky
trickle down his neck and under the collar of his sweatshirt. He rubbed his hand over his hair and got his hand
smeared with the gook.

"Bombs away!" came the command again, and Oscy
was hit.

"Bombs away! Bombs away!" The Flight Commander
picked up momentum and the eggs came cracking down,
aimed and not aimed, dropped delicately or hurled, cracking, exploding, splattering on to the ten boys below. From
some other room in the house a hearty version of "Praise
the Lord and Pass the Ammunition" was being battered
out on a tinny piano. The tune inspired others, and soon
there was a chorus of background music. "Over There"
. . . "Coming in on a Wing and a Prayer" . . . "This is
the Army, Mr. Jones" . . . "I left my Heart at the Stage
Door Canteen" . . . "The White Cliffs of Dover" . . . and
"When the Lights go on Again." A joyous musical background to the humiliation of the Pledges, who were
covered in the gruesome, slimy mess. They slipped and

skidded on the glutinous, egg-splattered floor as they tried to avoid the fast-falling missiles. With no place to hide, his clothes sodden with the filthy, clammy eggs, Hermie almost wished for a Mohawk haircut. If his mother could only see him now.

Afterwards, in the shower, trying to wash out the dried-on goo from his hair, Hermie told Oscy, "That's probably the worst they can do. I can't think of anything much more repulsive than that."

"I don't know," said Oscy. "That's probably just a build-up. I've heard some pretty gruesome tales. I should've stuck with my first fraternity choice. Maybe I'll go join the paratroopers instead."

"Egg's supposed to be good for the hair," said Hermie, looking on the bright side."

"Yeah, but it's lousy for the disposition," said Oscy. "This must've been what the Spanish Disposition was all about."

"Inquisition, dummy."

"That, too," grumbled Oscy.

Hermie was dried and dressed. "Hurry up, snail's pace, I'm starving. Let's go get something to eat."

"Yeah, okay, I'm starving, too. I'm ready. Whatta you feel like?"

"Bacon and eggs?" asked Hermie, ducking as Oscy's wet towel flew through the air.

20

Hermie read a speech of FDR's in History the next day. "The war effort must not be impeded by those who put their own selfish interests above the interests of the nation.

"It must not be impeded by a few bogus patriots who use the sacred freedom of the press to echo the sentiments of the propagandists in Tokyo and Berlin.

"And above all, it shall not be imperiled by the handful of noisy traitors—betrayers of America, betrayers of Christianity itself—would-be dictators, who in their hearts and souls have yielded to Hitlerism and would have this republic do likewise."

What a man! He sure knew how to string words together.

Hermie realized, all at once, that he was living history. The subject had always seemed such a bore, old battles and fusty chronicles. If it was recorded in history books it was dead, gone, over. But he suddenly realized that whatever happened in the world that very day, October 1, 1944, would be in the history books that his son would study in college. He was probably as much a part of history as Winston Churchill, FDR, Benjie, for instance, lobbing grenades in the Philippines, and Paulie Marcus, ten feet under, and his cousin, stagnating on Kiska, and Al, driving a tank in Europe. He doubted that he was an active part of history, as they were, but there had to be someone at home to report it, someone to write the history books. Roosevelt, for instance, *he'd* go down in history, and Hermie had seen him once, in person, on his way to Hyde Park from a parade on Wall Street. It was hard to put yourself in history, because it had always, until now, been something you studied. He'd assumed that you could only study something that was conclusive, like $2 + 2 = 4$. There was no way that could be changed. So you learned it, and you were supposed to remember it, because it was a fact. He'd kind of accepted history, the subject, in the same way, as a fact. Civilization, he'd believed, had reached its highest peak, and there he was, right on top of the heap, looking back on what was, saying, "Well, there were growing pains, but here we are at last, we've made it." Now it occurred to him that he wasn't at the apex at all. Everything was constantly changing around him. And he was right at the heart of it. Progress didn't come to an end when Hermie was born. They said in the papers that television was a fact already, and was all set to go into production after the war, and they were already making plans for exploring outer space. They'd probably never reach the moon but some scientists said it was a possibility. Maybe man wasn't even in his final form. Maybe by the time Hermie's grandson came to Conn U. he'd look completely different from the way man now appeared.

Hermie was bowled over by his revelation, so much so that he missed getting the class assignment and had to get it from one of the coeds after class.

Hermie's lofty thoughts had completely obscured any surmises about the next part of the Pledge initiations. The next step was scheduled for that evening. Oscy reminded him as he came into their room at Mrs. Gilhuly's.

"Y'know," Oscy greeted him, "this room isn't really so bad after all. Who needs a fraternity?"

"Oh, Christ, I'd forgotten. Tonight, isn't it?"

"We don't have to go."

"No, I've got one of those dumb consciences that makes me finish anything I start. You know me."

"What's that got to do with me?" Oscy asked. "My conscience never says a word."

"You don't understand. What I gotta complete, you gotta complete too. That's the deal I have with my conscience."

"I think I'm consorting with a crazy," Oscy told the toe of his clean white sweat sock.

"I noticed your conscience made you pick up your laundry," said Hermie.

"Well, you never know what I might have to take off. I thought I'd better start out clean," grumbled Oscy.

Actually it wouldn't have mattered, because the first thing the Pledges were asked to do was to remove their shoes and socks. Then they were marched across the football field, through the remains of Saturday's mud, to a telephone booth near the shuttered refreshment stand. Another officious senior with a paddle addressed the Pledges. "All right, men, are we ready? All shoes removed? Good. Now then, let us, in orderly fashion, march into this diving bell. One at a time, step lively."

Some of the other seniors began pushing the freshmen into the telephone booth. To get in they had to stand on each other's shoulders. Even doing it that way, only six managed to squeeze in. The four remaining tried to sneak away, Oscy and Hermie among them. The Telephone Man grabbed them by their shoulders and turned

them around to face the booth. "Room for four more,"
he called out brightly.

"Brains before beauty." Oscy pushed Hermie ahead.

"Gee, I don't have a nickel," Hermie demurred.

"Okay, I'll lend you," said Oscy.

"You!" the Telephone Man called out to Hermie.

"You talking to me, sir?"

"Yes, and your buddy."

"Me, sir?" said Oscy, surprised.

"Yes, the both of you. Let's go."

"I have terrible halitosis. It'll kill those poor boys."

"In you go or it's twenty paddles."

"Yes, I have an important call to make." Oscy thought
better of it.

Hermie and Oscy crammed in. Hermie had a muddy
foot in his face and one in his groin. Oscy was balanced
on the top of the others, with his face almost directly up
against the top of the booth, and only an inch of rarified
air to breathe. It was murder. The Telephone Man pushed
the door shut. Hands, feet and eyes bulged from within
the booth, ten humanoid fish trapped in an airless glass
bowl.

The Telephone Man shouted to the Pledges inside.
"Object of the game is: when the phone rings someone
must answer, find out which of you the phone call is for,
pass the receiver to that man and complete the call. There
is no time limit. Take as long as you must."

The gurgling and coughing from inside the booth
sounded as if it were coming from the terminal ward of
Montefiore Hospital. Air was at a premium and the boys
inside soon discovered that to survive they'd have to
breathe very little and very shallowly. The phone's ring
broke through the gurgles. It rang three or four times
before someone managed to answer it. It was Hermie. His
face up against the steamed glass, the heaviest freshman
in the whole school standing on his shoulders, a bullet-
shaped head slammed into his guts, someone's pickle-

flavored breath right in his face, Hermie coughed into the phone. "Hello? What? Yes. Whom do you wish to speak to? Who? What?" He began to cough again and couldn't stop. He managed to yell in anguish, "It's for Don Ameche! Yagggggghhhh!" The door was pushed open from inside and a gasping heap of boys spilled out on to the gravel. They lay like depleted balloons after a children's party, gagging in their efforts to get as much air into their lungs as fast as possible. The last man was barely out when the Telephone Man commiserated with them, very calmly.

"Too bad. Don Ameche didn't answer. So . . . we'll just have to try again. Line up." He steered them with his paddle, back into the fetid phone booth.

"Man, what I wouldn't give to be Clark Kent right now," one of the pledges gasped.

As the door closed on Oscy, almost gelding him, he gasped to Hermie, "You and I are gonna have a long talk about your fuckin' girlfriend."

Hermie soaked his feet for an hour back at Mrs. Gilhuly's. He couldn't seem to get the circulation back into them. He had so many bruises that even his bruises had bruises. He wondered if Julie knew the extent of the initiation rites at Pi Epsilon Tau. If she did, then she had a strong streak of sadism in her. Or maybe she just thought suffering was good for the soul. He wasn't at all sure he approved of the hazings and wondered how it would prove he was worthy of membership to the Secret Society if he were able to withstand all they had to throw at him. He could tell Oscy was wavering, and had to pay for lunch to get him to agree to go to the next day's session. It could get expensive if this went on much longer.

Oscy came in while Hermie was soaking his feet. He didn't say a word, just threw his books down on the floor, and himself on the bed and fell into instant slumber.

Hermie took off Oscy's Army boots and the once clean

sweat socks that were muddier inside than they were outside. Oscy never stirred.

Come to think of it, Hermie hadn't heard from Julie in a couple of days. Admittedly he'd been busy, with school and with the initiation stunts, but even so. She hadn't called him, even though he'd left messages at Gamma Upsilon for her. He'd talked to Janie and Jessica and Fay and Barbie, Lorraine and Mike. Mike?! Anyway, she hadn't returned any of his calls. Could be Miss Julie was doing a little hazing of her own. Whom *could* you trust?

21

Hermie tried reaching Julie again before he left for classes in the morning. He got Francine. She had a sexy voice. She sounded like Oscy's type. "Sorry, Julie's not here now. I could have her call you." Hermie suspected that Julie'd written down those words and had them pasted up by the phone at the sorority house. Every time he called he got almost exactly the same message. This time it had definitely sounded as if Francine were reading it. It just hadn't come out spontaneously enough. Just wait until he got hold of Julie. The thought changed shape even while he thought it, and ended with a totally different emphasis. Julie of the bobbing curls and the cute little ass. Ah, Julie!

That night the ten Pledges were told to strip naked and were led into a large room, bare of furniture. At one end of the room were two huge blocks of ice. At the far end were two hatracks. Oscy looked at Hermie and grimaced. What now?

Another one of the seniors was in charge. "I'm the Iceman," he introduced himself. Hermie thought that so far they could all have qualified for Hitler's cabinet. Goebbels would be a good name for this one. The Iceman had x-ray vision. He seemed to sense Hermie's thoughts and directed a steely glare at him. Hermie withered and hoped it didn't show. He needed his manhood like never before. The Pledges stood shivering while the Iceman took his time explaining what had to be done. "This game is called The Ice and the Olive."

"Game!" snorted Oscy, and received a round of machine-gun fire in his scrotum from the telepathic vision of Dr. Goebbels.

"Game," repeated Goebbels, scoring one up for their side. "Each team is comprised of five men and has one block of ice and one olive. The object of the game is for each man in turn to pick up the olive from the ice, run it around the hatrack at the far end of the room, and then re-deposit the olive on the ice where the next man will do likewise."

"Just like Cub Scouts," thought Hermie. "They're probably running out of stunts. This should be a piece of cake, except for frostbitten fingers maybe."

"All right. Line up," commanded Goebbels.

The Pledges lined up, five men behind each block of ice. Hermie could feel the cold emanating from it, causing goosebumps where no one should ever have goosebumps. It seemed almost too easy.

Oscy, shot down, but eternal, raised his hand.

"Yes? A question?" asked the Iceman.

"Begging your pardon, sir," Oscy said, having learned humility in the past few days, "but why are we naked?"

As if he just remembered, the Iceman clapped his hands together. "Ah, yes. I forgot to tell you. You may not use your hands to pick up the olive." Pause. "Or your toes." Pause. "Or your mouths." Pause. "Or your ears." Double-triple pause. "Or your noses."

Oscy asked it for all of them. "What's left?"

"Your ass," intoned the Iceman, in tones of purest dulcet.

"You're kidding," said Oscy.

"And," Goebbels continued, "should you drop the olive along the way, you must pick it up in the same manner in which you just picked it up in the first place. Losing team members get twenty-five whacks with the sacred paddle."

"Cub Scouts was never like this," thought Hermie.

"I should point out," added their Mentor, "that both olives are the same size, so there will be no advantage to either team. Thirty seconds to prepare your team order."

The lines that had already formed before the news was out, quickly unformed. Nobody wanted to go first. As a matter of ice cold fact, nobody wanted to go at all. There was a deal of bustling as each man tried to be the last in the line. Hermie wondered if he could pull the stunt he sometimes used in gym class in high school. As each boy would rejoin the line after taking his turn at jumping the horse, or climbing the rope, or walking along a parallel bar, or whatever idiotic thing the gym teacher had thought up for them that day, Hermie would push the boy in front of him, so that *he* was always at the end of the line. That way he never had to take a turn. The gym teacher never found out. Of course he was short sighted. Hermie received A regularly in Physical Education. Somehow Hermie had a feeling the Field Marshall here wasn't short sighted, also the other boys weren't about to let Hermie off the hook.

"Go on, Hermie," said Oscy. "You were always a great lead-off man." Oscy got behind him and pushed him forward.

"Forget it," said Hermie.

"You go, Oscy," one of the other Pledges said.

"Screw," said Oscy.

"All in favor of Oscy going first . . ." the same Pledge appealed to the team. They all raised their hands, including Hermie.

Oscy looked at his heretofore friend. "Et tu, Hermie?"

"Bet your ass," said Hermie.

The contest began. Oscy was forced to go first for their team. He approached the block of ice cautiously, facing it, then decided that wasn't a good angle, so he turned around. He tried sitting down on the olive, and rose with such a shriek of horror that the other eleven Pledges froze without benefit of ice. He tried again, this time somehow managing to get the olive between the cheeks of his ass before he became a permanent part of the block of ice. He started to hobble down the room, finding that a duck-waddle was his best bet. He flat-footed it down the room, keeping a tight hold on his sphincter muscle. There was absolute silence in the room, nothing like the excitement that usually attended a race of this kind. Oscy was almost back to the ice when he felt the olive slipping. He gritted his teeth and dove for the ice, sliding across it just as the olive fell out and settled back in its place, like a contented egg deposited by a frozen duck.

Hermie was third in line. He'd been watching carefully, trying to judge, from example and logic, what the best approach might be. He figured that the ice was probably melting by now and wouldn't be that cold. He was wrong. It was colder. Much colder. The olive had picked up an icy gloss by that time and it took him a century or two before he could get a grasp on it. By the time he did he found that his ass was so numb that he had no control of the muscles there, just when he needed them most. The most irritating part of the whole thing was that when you felt the olive stuck there, like a frozen bullet, the obvious and natural impulse was to try to expel it, which was exactly what you didn't want to do. Three times he dropped the olive. The third time it dropped between the block of ice and the wall, a very narrow area. Hermie had to scrunch down between the ice and the wall to get at the damned olive. Not only were his ass muscles frozen into immobility, the whole side of his body that was next to the ice was paralyzed. He finally got a grip on the thing and made the rest of the trip in a severely deformed position, half of his body being useless. He wondered what the effects of freezing were on the balls. They definitely weren't erotic. He hoped ice didn't have the same effect as the mumps.

After his turn was over, he was in such an uncomfortable state that he hardly noticed how the rest of the team made out. He could remember one agonizing half-hour when Marty couldn't get the idea at all, and the rest of the team had to stand around, like ice-carvings, trying to give him suggestions.

Sometime after the end of the Third World War the contest came to a close. No one remembered exactly how it came out, because nobody wanted to. It was never written in the history books, but there was a whole group of men, to be found in many fields of endeavor, who later in life shared two things in common; they were graduates of the University of Connecticut and they took their martinis without olives. Psychiatrists who studied the phenomenon could come to no amicable agreement as to the reason for such unusual behavior, especially since all the men in the group had developed unbreakable memory blocks about the month of October in the year 1944.

On his way home, Hermie called Gamma Upsilon. He left a message for Julie. "Tell her don't call me, I'll call her."

Back at Mrs. Gilhuly's, Oscar and Herman lay on their stomachs on their beds. Neither of them made any effort to move. Neither of them could. Even their voices seemed to have been affected.

When the telephone rang on the landing outside their

room, neither of them made any attempt to answer it. After a few moments, the Baron poked his head in. "It's for you, Herman, and it's after ten o'clock."

"Tell 'em I died," Hermie said, unable to raise himself off the bed. It was probably Julie and he wanted to punish her.

Oscy finally broke the glacial silence in the room. Hermie could hardly hear him. He had to lean forward to catch his words. "This fraternity crap is beginning to lose its charm. I've got frostbite, Hermie. Frostbite of the ass."

"You're lucky. I don't even have an ass."

"Those twenty-five whacks didn't help my emotions."

"If crazy Marty didn't drop the olive we'd have won . . . took him half an hour to get back in the race."

"That kid has no coordination. None whatsoever."

"Oh, well," said Hermie, philosophically. "Win a few, lose a few."

They both started laughing and couldn't stop. It wasn't amusement as much as hysteria. Mrs. Gilhuly banged on their door twice before they were able to stop. They both slept the sleep of the just. The just-defrosted.

Partially recovered, Oscy and Hermie stood with the other Pledges in the living room of the fraternity house. It was a handsome room, Hermie had to admit, wood-panelled, comfortable chairs, good lighting, gentleman's club atmosphere, but still. . . .

All the senior members, Hitler, Goering, Goebbels, Himmler and their General Staff stood in a semi-circle, paddles at the ready.

"You know," whispered Oscy. "I think the War Effort could benefit from the experience of these guys. They must have been trained in Berchtesgaden."

"Sshh," said Hermie. "Haven't you learned when to keep quiet yet?"

The President began to speak. "Rarely, if ever, do we choose to have any of our initiation activities go beyond the hallowed confines of our fraternity house."

"They wouldn't dare," thought Hermie. "They'd be arrested."

"However, this year, thanks to the ingenuity of Brother Samuel here. . . ." Goering inclined his head. The other senior members applauded. The Pledges, afraid *not* to, afraid *to,* kind of "Hm-hmmmed" apprehensively. With this kind of a build-up it had to be good.

The President went on. "We are going to make an exception. Here we have . . . ten little bells." He picked up a box from the desk in front of him and shook it. It jingled. Bells all right. "Yes, dear Pledges, ten little bells. One for each of you." He shook the box again. "Pretty?"

No one spoke.

"I asked if they were pretty."

The Pledges rushed in with appreciative "Prettys, Beautifuls and Lovelys" with the right amount of enthusiasm.

"Thank you. Such rewarding enthusiasm. Now then, in a moment, each of you will have a bell of his own, one of *these.*" He jingled the goddamned box again. "Key of C, I believe. And it will be attached, dear Pledges, to your own family jewels, making each of you, if you're all there, look somewhat like a small pawnshop." He opened the box and displayed the ten little bells. "And the bell will remain attached until your initiation is concluded. Oh, yes . . . one more thing."

"Of course . . ." breathed Oscy.

The President brought out another, smaller box. "To your individual musical instruments there will also be attached this small tag so that *everyone* can play on you his or her favorite song." He picked up one of the tags and displayed it. "As you can see, there is a small, two-word directive on this tag. It reads: 'Pull me!' Yes, that's what it reads. 'Pull me!' The tag, as you might imagine. He smiled beatifically. "Some of you, I see, are ahead of me. The tag will be hung on the outside, over your belt buckle, and must always be in full view of the public. It must always be readily available to all music lovers . . . to see, and read . . . and act upon."

There was a deathly silence in the room. Not Berchtesgaden, thought Hermie, Ivan the Terrible's torture chamber. This guy could probably've taught Attila a thing or two.

The Gestapo smiled conspiratorially at each other. Hermie expected them to shake hands and clap each other on the back at any minute.

The Headman summed up. "This is the first time for our little musical game and, if all goes well, we would like to add it to our repertoire."

"Along with the Rack and the Wheel," hissed Oscy.

"So don't let us down, fellows. Don't let yourselves down, n'est ce pas?"

Hermie had always hated people who said things like 'n'est ce pas' and 'tres bien.' He didn't change his mind. Now he had concrete reasons, not just vague theorizings. He'd been having misgivings about this whole fraternity business before this last trial but now he was ready to throw in the towel. He was bored with it because it all seemed so fucking trivial. What did it have to do with anything? And if belonging to a fraternity meant associating with people like these Gestapos, who needed it. He knew that once the initiations were over they'd seem like different people and he'd probably get along with them okay, but he'd never have stayed with it if it hadn't've been for Julie's insistance that they *had* to belong to a fraternity. The rooms were more pleasant than the ones they rented at the Gilhulys, the food was great, the rules were looser, but still, all this humiliation. However, it was too late to back down now and Hermie took his place in line for the final humiliation, the ceremonial Tying-on-of-the-Bell. His was tied with a blue ribbon, baby blue. It didn't really hurt, just made him feel like a freak at the circus.

22

Hermie and Oscy walked, albeit a little stiffly to their next class. They tried to hide their 'Pull me!' tags under long sweaters, but there was no way. They hung like flashing signals over their belt buckles. Hermie's eyes darted around, hoping no one had, or would, notice the tag.

"I wonder if we can put in for a Purple Heart?" asked Oscy.

"A purple what?"

"Sure changes a man's way of life. When this thing is over I'm gonna get hold of good old brother Samuel and I'm gonna play "Canadian Capers" on his . . ."

Hermie prodded him in the ribs.

"What?" hissed Oscy.

"Dead ahead. Bandits at 12 o'clock." Coming toward them, directly in their path, were three senior Pi Epsilon men.

"You cut to the right," said Oscy. "I'll cut to the left. Good luck."

"Roger," said Hermie.

No good. They'd been spotted. One of the seniors roared out a "Hey! Hold it there!"

Both Oscy and Hermie stopped and pointed innocently at themselves. "Who, me?"

The frat men motioned them to come together again, which they did. Three seniors gathered around Hermie and Oscy.

"Say," said one of them, "Look at this cute little thing."

"What does it say?" asked the second.

"Why, I believe it says 'Pull me!' " said the third.

"Then why don't we pull?"

"Let's."

Gaily, and without any consideration for the sensitivity of Herm's and Oscar's tender parts, they executed a fairly acceptable "Chopsticks."

"Hey, Hermie," piped Oscy, in a high falsetto, "I think something happened to my voice." He clutched his throat.

"I always had my doubts about you, anyway," said Hermie, recovering his sense of humor and dodging Oscy's threatening paw at the same time.

When the seniors were well out of earshot, Oscy narrowed his eyes. "I'm going to live through this for one reason, and one reason only . . . so I can get my own back when I'm a senior. I'm planning tortures even now."

"You should only live so long," said Hermie, blessing him with a tin fork he'd carried out of the cafeteria.

When Hermie'd stopped calling Julie, she'd started calling him. He'd refused the first two calls, having Oscy give back with the "Sorry, he's not here, I could have him call you" routine. But he wasn't able to keep it up for very long. Finally, he broke down and called her. This time she answered the phone.

"Julie?"

"Hermie?"

"Uh-huh."

"Uh-huh."

"Brilliant conversationalists, aren't we?" said Hermie.

"I have other talents," said Julie.

"I remember. Where've you been?"

"Where've *I* been? You didn't return my last two calls."

"Before which you didn't return my last two billion calls."

"I was digging in my Victory Garden."

"Right, I heard."

"No, I was wrapping Bundles for Britain."

"Sure you weren't selling War Bonds?"

"Unh-huh, I was too busy taking my place in Civil Defense."

"But you *were* giving your generous support to the American Red Cross."

"Definitely. I've been a very busy little war worker. What've you been doing?"

"Swinging on a star, of course."

"I heard it was more like clang-clang-clanging on the trolley," Julie laughed.

"That's not very funny, Julie. And while we're on the subject of fraternities . . ."

"Listen, Hermie, I think I hear my bath water spilling over."

"Let it."

"Yes Hermie."

"What made you choose Pi Epsilon Tau?"

"Why do you ask?"

"You don't happen to have a thing against men, do you?"

"Why, Hermie, how could you think such a thing. Anyway, I used to go with a guy from there . . . Pi Epsilon."

"You almost used to go with a Pledge from there," Hermie said.

"Was it really that bad?" Julie asked. "They said they'd go easy on you."

"Oh, they went easy on us, like the bombs fell easy on London. Yes, it was really that bad. Julie, it was awful. And it's not even over yet."

"I'm sorry, Hermie, I really am. I know you'll enjoy it once you're a member. They have the best kitchen in college, and definitely the best parties."

"Tell me, Julie, am I a little whacky, or have you been avoiding me during this whole initiation week?"

"Who, me?"

"Yes, innocent, you."

She giggled over the phone. Hermie saw her face in front of him and immediately forgave her everything. "Well, I thought maybe it would be better if you concentrated on one thing at a time."

"I think you were more afraid that Oscy and I might jointly mutilate you, piece by beautiful piece of that gorgeous body."

"Yes, that too, I must admit."

"All right, you're forgiven. But only if you meet me in the library in ten minutes."

"But my bath . . ."

"Let Francine have it."

"How do you know Francine?"

"You'd be surprised."

"Well, I do have to get a book."

"Ten minutes?"

"Okay, O Great One, I trot like Fala to your command."

"Ten minutes."

"Ten minutes."

"Kiss?"

"Kiss-kiss. Mm. That felt good. Ten minutes."

Hermie waited outside the library for Julie, because he

couldn't kiss her inside, and he wanted to kiss her very much. It was a cold evening, but her lips were warm and sweet as she came into his arms. She felt almost too fragile to hold. Hermie held his long arms around her, protecting her from whatever unknown dangers might be lurking on the library steps.

Inside they had to whisper. The librarian, a caricature of a typically fusty old maid, with streaked grey hair, horn-rimmed specs and non-functional large breasts, had a thing against young love and frowned on it whenever it reared its ugly head. She'd once told someone she'd gone to school with Greer Garson, at some obscure English college. She had long hairs protruding from her nose, and looked not at all like Greer Garson.

"I'm not sure I share your enthusiasm for the fraternity life," whispered Hermie.

"Disillusioned?"

"Dismembered would be a better word."

"I wouldn't worry about it if I were you." Julie pecked him on the cheek in the History section.

"Swell. I wouldn't worry about it if I were *you*, either."

"Ah, here it is. English History." She lifted an enormous tome off the shelf. "Whuuf. Is it ever big. And such a small country. Anyway, you sure you have the time to help me with this?"

Hermie took the big book from her. "Sure I'm sure."

"Wasn't it smart of me to pick a genius for a boyfriend?"

"You'd've been better off with a weight-lifter," Hermie puffed.

"I like you better."

"Thanks. But I can't take the exam for you."

"Oh, I'll pass."

"How do you know?"

"Because I always do. One way or another . . . things work out for me. *You* know that."

"How much of this are you required to know?"

"I've got a note on it somewhere. I think I have to know about two Richards and an Edward."

"Which Richards and which Edward?"

"Or maybe it was Henry. Ah . . ." She found her notebook. "Two Richards, one Henry and one Elizabeth . . . or is it a Victoria?" She smiled at Hermie, who was taking it all very seriously. "Right. Two Richards, one Henry, one Victoria . . . and a Hermie. Kiss me, you fool." She moved closer to him.

"Here?" asked Hermie, looking around.

"Anywhere you like," said Julie, holding up her face. She hugged him, kissed him, and suddenly in the silence of the reading room a small bell could be heard to tinkle.

"Merry Christmas," giggled Julie, while the librarian, wreathed in disapproval, shushed them loudly. She managed to stop them talking, but there wasn't a thing she could do about the bell, at least nothing that she'd ever read about in her librarian's manual.

Hermie spent most of the next hour looking at Julie. Julie spent most of the next hour looking at Hermie. Henry and Elizabeth had perforce to look at each other. Never had History proved such an aphrodisiac. Hermie reached out to stroke Julie's hair. She caught his hand, and carrying it to her lips, kissed him in the palm. As she bent her head to the big history book, he parted the hair at the back of her neck and kissed the soft, vulnerable skin there. She smelled like apricots. The damned bell began jingling, like Victory in Europe. Julie moved closer, and under the table, reached out her hand to stop the tintinnabulation. Hermie almost died right there in the library. He was afraid he'd never be able to walk again. He looked over toward the librarian, where she sat so staid and virginal. He feared that any minute the table might levitate up to the ceiling and out into the night, not quite under its own steam. The librarian, directing a scornful gaze at Hermie, spat out at him, "Young man, put down that table at once. You don't know where it's been!" Hermie laughed at the scene in his imagination. His mother always used to say that if he picked up a lost toy truck or a kitten in the street.

"Julie, do you think we could get the hell out of here? I'm getting claustrophobia." Among other things.

"Well, I'm done with Henry and Victoria, but I haven't quite finished Hermie yet," she teased.

"Julie, you don't know the half of it," he said.

"Mm," she said appreciatively. "I think I do."

Just then the librarian's handbell, much louder and less melodious than Hermie's little jingle, startled them both out of a couple years' growth.

Julie started to giggle. "Listen to her jingle! Who'd've thought the old girl had it in her!"

"Library's closing in ten minutes," the librarian intoned, as librarians are wont to do. "Please return all reference books to the shelves." She flicked the lights to make it official.

Hermie banged Julie's big history book shut and handed it to her. "Here, you put it back. I don't have the strength." He tried to think flaccid as Julie returned the book to its shelf. She was still smiling when she came back to collect him.

"Let's go neck," she offered.

"Actually I was hoping you'd have some more history for me to help you with."

"I do, but not here." She led the way as Hermie painfully followed her out of the library, past the librarian's disapproving glare, into the cold of the October night, which worked wonders for Hermie's awkward condition.

He walked Julie back to her sorority house. There was a corrugated-iron Quonset hut, like part of an airplane hanger parked on the back lawn of the building. It was supposed to be a repository for tools for the house's Victory Garden, but had become a repository for a great many other things since its official installation. Julie took Hermie's hand and led him into the farthest, darkest corner of the hut, where they bumped smack into living, breathing . . . heavy breathing flesh. "Sorry," Julie whispered, moving along to the opposite corner, which was also occupied. It was impossible to tell just how many couples were doing what to whom right there in the Victory Garden hut. They finally found a spot that seemed to be temporarily unoccupied. "Hey, no-man's land!" whispered Julie loudly, claiming it for them. Hermie pushed Julie up against the metal of the hut's wall and kissed her. He put his hands under her sweater. Her skin was warm and unbelievably soft. Hermie felt himself drowning in her sweetness. He opened his coat and drew her body against his. She fitted in all the crucial places. He nuzzled her neck, then pulled her sweater up until he could touch the tip of a sharply-defined nipple with his tongue. He felt her shudder against him. Suddenly the heavy breathing all around him began to work on his erection. He felt desensitized, almost as if he were part of an overall plan, like one of the cogs in Charlie Chaplin's "Modern Times." There were too many couples around, too much fumbling, too much nuzzling, too much petting, too much sucking, nibbling and patting. It sounded like a Chicago stockyard on auction day. Apart from everything else he was afraid any minute that he might touch the wrong breast, kiss the wrong lips. He held Julie quietly in his arms for a few minutes, then said, "Let's get out of here."

She seemed to know what it was that bothered him. At the door of the house she stood on tiptoe and kissed him on the nose. "I think I love you, Herman Green," she said, and ran in and up the stairs.

Hermie walked home in a daze. Sex was a funny thing. You could be so turned on one minute, and so turned off the next. All those guys who talked about "doing it" as if it were an athletic feat were full of shit. That had nothing to do with love. He wanted to make love to Julie;

he didn't want to "make her" or "do it" to her. He didn't suppose he could ever explain that to Oscy, but then he wasn't even going to try.

The lecture room was stuffy and crowded as usual. Hermie was doing his best to stay awake, as were most of the others in the room. The non-stop drama professor was rambling on but had lost most of his listeners long ago to their own daydreams.

". . . keeping in mind that the old balladeers took their songs from one town to the next, was it any wonder that new stanzas were improvised and added along the way. Was it?"

Since he already knew the answer, no one volunteered to help him out. He answered his own question, as everyone knew he would. "Of course not. Nor were these added verses necessarily true. For many of the lyrics were little more than fiction. Why do I say that?"

From somewhere near the back of the room a little bell jingled.

"I'll tell you why . . ." the teacher droned on.

Hermie looked around the room and caught the eye of one of the ten Pledges. The boy winked at Hermie.

". . . because though much of these ballads are accepted as gospel, it becomes patently obvious that they have no basis in truth." The professor cleared his throat and had a peppermint.

Another jingle from another part of the room. Hermie grinned and looked around, locating the second Pledge. The two bells jingled intermittently, unnoticed by the narcissistic professor, who was fixated on his own voice. He'd have rambled on through the Battle of Britain, thought Hermie. He'd probably go right on through Armageddon without ever noticing that the rest of the world had disintegrated around him. Like a tower of words, he'd stand, armored in impervious prattle, unharmed, still holding forth, while cities fell, people died, whole continents were swallowed back into the ocean, quibbling while Rome burned.

"And yet," the professor droned on, "how many of the laws and legends with us today are founded on the accepted veracity of these very untruths merely because they rhymed and could be set to a pleasant music?"

Hermie took the professor's remarks as a cue and, without reflecting anything on his face, tunefully joined his bell to those of his colleagues already jingling in harmony. Together the three reached new heights of syncopation as the oblivious professor sucked on his peppermint and sounded forth on his subject.

As the period came to an end, the jingling bells continued their pleasant music out into the corridors. Soon they were joined by other Pledges, all joined in one joyful carillon, until the whole school rocked with the sound of bells, topped by the tolling of the giant bell in the bell tower. Bong! Bong! Bong! Up in the tower the Hunchback of Notre Dame, borrowed for the occasion, laughed as he tolled and grunted, then howled at the top of his lungs, "Sanctuary! Sanctuary!"

23

Thank the Lord it was all over. The initiation had ended. All the Pledges had made it. The goddamned bells had been ceremoniously united and handed as mementos to the victorious Pledges. Oscy was thinking of having his bronzed, along with its recent neighbors, because he seemed to have developed a worrying numbness. He didn't feel he had that many assets that he could afford to lose one of them and was thinking seriously of consulting a veterinarian.

In a wilder moment, Oscy suggested a party to celebrate. He and Hermie sneaked a dozen quart bottles of beer up the stairs past the ever alert Mrs. Gilhuly, who'd've made a first rate Civil Defense air-raid warden, since she obviously never slept. For food they had pretzels, and potato chips. For girls they used imagination and a good deal of braggadocio. Oscy had suggested smuggling up a couple under his coat, but Hermie didn't think it would work. One of the boys had a bottle of gin that a wild uncle had sent him as a graduation present. He'd been hoarding it ever since, hiding it under his underwear at home, with his dirty pictures, so that his mother wouldn't find it. His mother had packed his bags when he left for college. He had a friend call her on the telephone while she was packing so that he could get her out of the room long enough to stick the bottle under his clothes in the suitcase.

The boys sat around on whatever available surfaces there were and drank their way slowly through the beer and the gin. Oscy was the life of the party. He was the only one who managed to remember the whole joke, punch-line as well, which was something Hermie, for all his intellectual superiority, envied him.

"Didya hear the one about the sailor who was trying to make a girl? 'No,' she said, 'last time I went out with the Navy I was torpedoed and now I'm a Troop carrier'!"

Oscy laughed the loudest at his own jokes, and shushed himself just as loudly.

"I heard that in London, the material they make women's underpants with is so thin that they sell 'em with the slogan 'One Yank and they're off!' Get it. One yank!" He guffawed loudly. Hermie stuffed a pillow into his face.

Oscy pulled away the pillow. "Hear what Bob Hope said when he heard FDR was going to run for a fourth term? He said 'I've always voted for Roosevelt as President. My father always voted for Roosevelt for President. My grandfather always voted for Roosevelt for President.'"

Hermie interrupted the laughter. "The Londoners call the buzz-bombs Bob Hopes, short for 'Bob down and Hope for the best!' "

Oscy began laughing in advance at another story of his own and wouldn't stop until Jerry Wild, one of the other Pledges threatened to stick a beer bottle down his throat. "If it's so funny, tell it, then," said Jerry.

"Well, there were these two men in a railway train

and one man had a banana stuck in his ear. After a while, the other man leaned over and said, very politely, 'Excuse me, sir, but why do you have a banana stuck in your ear?' The other man said, 'I beg your pardon, sir, what did you say?' The first man spoke a bit louder. 'Excuse me, sir, but why do you have a banana stuck in your ear?' The second man excused himself again. 'Sorry, sir, what did you say?' The first man yelled, real loud, 'EXCUSE ME, SIR, BUT WHY DO YOU HAVE A BANANA STUCK IN YOUR EAR?' The second man shook his head and leaned over to the first man. 'I'm so sorry, old man,' he said, 'You'll have to excuse me. You see I can't hear too well, because I have a banana stuck in my ear.' "

"Hey," said Marty, reminded by the last story, "knock, knock."

"Who's there?" asked Oscy.

"Bananas."

"Bananas who?"

"Knock, knock."

"Who's there?"

"Bananas."

"Bananas who?"

"Knock, knock."

"Who's there."

"Orange."

"Orange who?"

"Orange you glad I didn't say bananas?" howled Marty. The Pledges dissolved into hysteria at the stupidity of the story. Suddenly there was a knock, knock on the door.

"Who's there?" sang out Oscy.

"Mrs. Gilhuly."

"Mrs. Gilhuly who?" Oscy yelled.

She refused to play the game. She'd been knocking for five minutes before anyone had heard her. She flung the door open and stood there, framed in the doorway, an overaged avenging Angel.

Oscy maneuvered his way across the room and, standing in front of her, wavering only slightly, he grabbed the initiative, in the true Oscy manner. "Mrs. Gilhuly, I'm so glad you could come." He bowed from the waist and had to be supported by Hermie or he would've fallen over. "My good friend here, Hermie, and me . . . I . . . would like to tender our resignation to you. We will no longer be dwelling in your humble abode . . . after the first of the month."

"You'll no longer be dwelling in my humble abode after the first of the morning," Mrs. Gilhuly fixed them with an icy stare.

"The pleasure was all yours," Oscy bowed again and fell gallantly to the floor, causing the biggest laugh of the evening.

The next morning, Hermie and Oscy, suffering considerably with pachyderm-sized hangovers, moved their stuff into the Pi Epsilon Tau house, where a room had been rapidly readied for them. It was a great room on the third floor, overlooking the whole campus. It was much bigger than their old room at Mrs. Gilhuly's, and much more tastefully decorated. The furniture was light oak. They each had a chest of drawers, a desk, a nightstand, night lamp and, of course, a bed. Everything matched, nothing like the thrown-together hodge-podge they'd been living with.

"Now this is a room to bring a girl to," said Oscy, surveying it with delight.

"I'm sorry to inform you, old fellow, but unfortunately, in that particular area, the same silly rules still apply."

"You're kidding! You mean I got a frozen ass and a permanently numbed pair of testicles for nothing?"

"You've got to admit it's a better deal," Hermie said.

"Yeah, but . . ." Oscy had known about the rule. It was just an obligatory objection. He had to have his daily grumble.

There was a dance planned for that evening. Oscy figured the best way to plan for it was to sleep, which he did while Hermie unpacked and put away their stuff. Hermie had learned that if he wanted to live in any kind of order, he'd have to be mother to Oscy, hang up his clothes, pick up his books, all that stuff. It was a pain in the neck, but worth it. It wasn't that Hermie was so neat, just that Oscy was such a slob. After a while Oscy's mess would encroach on Hermie, then it was like living in a slide area. You never knew when the rocks were going to descend.

24

The Pi Epsilon House looked totally different now that they were members. It was much warmer, less forbidding. The seniors, too, as Hermie had suspected, were just ordinary guys. They even served punch and food to the new members as if they'd never stood over them with paddles in that very same room. Hermie looked for signs of those huge blocks of ice, or of the dozens of smashed eggs in the hallway. Nothing. Those things might well have been figments of Hermie's imagination, for all the trace he could find of them. That was the best thing about bad memories. They faded pretty fast. Nothing seemed quite so bad in retrospect. Hermie loved words like retrospect. He was trying to increase his vocabulary. So far he hadn't dared to try out most of his new words, except in his thoughts, because he wasn't sure of their pronunciation. He'd started to use an occasional new word in his newspaper reports. A couple had looked quite impressive in print.

The house was gaily decorated for the party with balloons and streamers. A large sign on one wall read: WELCOME NEW BROTHERS . . . PI EPSILON TAU . . . 1944.

Hermie and Julie were dancing very close. He was singing in her ear, with the record on the phonograph, "A kiss is just a kiss, a sigh is just a sigh. . . ."

Julie was wearing something terribly slinky and very sexy in wine-colored velvet. She had a large flat bow in matching velvet gathering her curls together at the back of her head. She had to be by far the best-looking girl there, by a million miles, which didn't displease Hermie at all. He'd noticed a couple of seniors eyeing her speculatively and kept her very close to him, as close at least as a constantly recurring condition would allow. A number of other boys were plagued with the same symptom, boys being boys and girls being girls. It tended to cause quite a bit of ass-bumping as the boys steered their girls around the crowded room. Hermie supposed that when you got older you didn't get quite so excited so fast. He'd spent many hours studying couples in movies and never, never had he seen a guy having an erection. Of course, it wasn't real in the movies. Someone'd told him that when they kissed in the movies it was really faked. It sure looked like the real thing, and a fellow had to be real close to a girl to even fake a kiss. There were so many questions like that that Hermie would've liked to have asked somebody. But he didn't know who'd have the answers. It was hardly the kind of thing you wrote in a letter to *Photoplay*.

Another thing he wondered about was why you always seemed to get an erection at the worst possible moment. Like when you came to your stop on the subway, or when you had to get up to write on the board at school. Hermie had solved the subway problem part way by carrying a newspaper with him when he traveled. It didn't stop the erection, or the pain when you had to walk the length of the car with an enormous lump in your pants, but it did serve some kind of a camouflage, so at least not everybody else knew about it. The school thing was different. Carrying a newspaper around the corridors didn't make much sense, and the irritating part about it was that you wouldn't get the erection until just before you knew you were going to have to get up to recite or something. He'd try frantically to think of something scary, like being in a street fight, in big danger. Sometimes that worked, but other times that vision got all tangled up with other ones, erotic ones, and then he was sunk.

Once they'd had a young pretty teacher in high school teaching, of all things, biology. Half the class would sit there with hard-ons, glazed-eyed as she discussed reproduction in amoebas. She might have been discussing pornography. Then there was the thing he'd tried from the Frank Harris book. Someone, probably Oscy, had managed to get a bootlegged copy of *Frank Harris: My Life and Loves.* They'd passed it all around the neighborhood, until it disappeared one day and was never seen again. In this book Harris told how he was plagued by constant erection as a kid, and to combat it, had tied a piece of string around his limp member. Whenever it tried to rise of its own accord, the string would get tight and down it would go. Hermie thought that sounded like a marvelous idea, so one day he tried it. All was well until that night when he went to a movie. There was a rather steamy scene in the film, someone removed a stocking; the string began to get tighter and tighter. Soon he was in terrible pain. He reached in to try and loosen the string, but it was much too tight. He tried to calm himself but the action on the screen was hot as hell. He tried to tell himself the girl wasn't attractive, not his type, she was flat-chested, ugly, but nothing worked. It was half an hour before the Pathe News came on and he was able to breathe again. Hopefully all that stuff would drop into place when you reached maturity, whenever *that* was.

"Who's Oscy dancing with?" Julie asked, interrupting his rather personal reverie.

"Georgette something-or-other."

"Is it serious?"

"No, she's just here for the occasion. His real girl . . . doesn't dance. Though I think . . . she does a lot of . . . *other* things."

"I'll tell you a secret. If he wants her, Georgette, I mean, he's home free. I know that look."

"I don't think he wants her."

The record changed to "Paper Doll" and Hermie steered Julie out of the room on to the porch. It was cool, but not too cool, a welcome relief from the overheated dance room. They could hear the music from inside. The moon was shining. Hermie put his arm around Julie. And it was good. He was just going to kiss her when she spoke.

"Hermie . . . is there something you want to give me?"

Hermie reacted by holding her closer. Indeed there was. "What?" he asked, thinking it was a rhetorical question.

"You know what," she whispered.

"Well, yes, but . . ." He looked at her face. They were talking about different things. "Oh, you mean this?" He took off his fraternity pin and handed it to her.

"No, no, no," she said disdainfully. "I've got enough of those."

"Then . . . what?"

"Your . . . bell."

He laughed and pulled her to him in a bear-hug.

"Do you have it with you?"

"Cut it out. We don't have to wear them any more."

"But you *do* have it with you."

"I have it. Will you stand back!" He brought out the bell from his pocket. "All present and accounted for." He rang it, then handed it to her. "With this bell I thee ring."

"Mm, thanks." She kissed him, ringing the bell simultaneously. "Actually, the whole thing was part of a Pavlov experiment. Now, every time I kiss you, you'll hear a bell ring."

"I didn't need the conditioning. Every time I kiss you I hear bells anyway."

"I've always wanted a fraternity man's bell. It's a dream come true." She jingled it gaily. "Where do I wear it?"

"That's your problem. *I* had no trouble."

They hugged as the colored light ball from the dance room inside flashed them red and blue and gold.

Just then the music changed to "Mairzy Doats." Hermie held Julie at arm's length. "I hate to tell you this, Julie," he said seriously.

"What is it?"

"They're playing our song."

"Mairzy Doats?"

"Mairzy Doats."

"How'd that get to be our song?"

"It was playing the first time we met, in the diner."

"We met in the newspaper office."

"True, but nothing was playing. So we had to wait. That's the rule . . . the first song that's played when we're together . . . that becomes *our* song."

"Mairzy Doats?"

"And little lambs eat ivy."

"Well, I won't have it."

"Baby, you got it," Hermie said, taking her inside to fully appreciate the music.

Oscy grabbed Hermie's arm as he went by the food table. "Listen, Hermie, I got this problem."

"Yes, I noticed."

"No, I'm supposed to meet Glenda at midnight and this Georgette is coming on like gangbusters. What'll I do?"

"Oscy, a man of your experience, can't you juggle with two hands at once?"

"Hermie, this is serious."

"I got it! Tell her you're really Lamont Cranston and you have to leave. It's an emergency." Hermie took Julie and led her into a modified Lindy to *their* song. Oscy aimed daggers at the back of Hermie's neck, but couldn't draw blood. Just then Georgette came back from the powder room and took him possessively by the arm.

"Let's dance, Oscy. I'm having a wonderful time!" she giggled, intimating that there was plenty more to come.

Oscy sighed and followed her onto the dance floor. The phonograph swung into a slowed-down version of "Too-ra-loo-ra-loo-ra." Oscy groaned almost audibly. The lights were dimmed down for the last dance of the night. It was the unwritten law that when you danced the last dance with a girl, you had to take her home. The thought of all that it entailed was almost too much for Oscy. He remembered an advertisement he'd seen in a magazine, of a soldier loading the breach of a machine-gun, under enemy fire. The caption under the picture read: "*He* won't dodge this—Don't *you* dodge this." It was a Buy War Bonds ad. Oscy let out a deep sigh. All right, he wouldn't dodge his responsibility. There were so many men away at the front. American womanhood wouldn't go hungry while Oscy still had his strength. Glenda would just have to wait. He took a deep breath and pushed Georgette toward the door. "All right, girl, beddy-bye time. Get your coat." Georgette giggled and pushed her ass against him as he steered her through the crowd. Oscy felt life. Maybe it wouldn't be so bad after all. "Never in the field of human conflict was so much done to so many by so few," was the way he paraphrased it to himself. Great man, that Churchill.

25

Hermie tried to study in his room. He had a biology test, and unfortunately the biology he'd been studying recently wasn't going to help him. Oscy never seemed to spend any time at his desk. Hermie had threatened to rent it out. Oscy's life was one perpetual social round; girls, beer, late night stag parties. In between social engagements he'd manage to make an occasional class, but there was never any chance of running into him at the library. Hermie had asked him how he intended to get through semester finals, and realized, almost as soon as he asked, that Oscy's refusal to study was a kind of death wish. He really wanted to flunk out, so he could say, "Look, I told you so. I should've gone into the Army in the first place." You couldn't talk to Oscy about anything serious. That was just Hermie's private thought. College was a pretty nice place to be, except for that grudging little thought that kept popping up when you least needed it, that maybe the Pacific Theater was really the place you ought to be. Hermie had a feeling that his father was probably mentally holding his breath, waiting for some kind of announcement from Hermie. His father didn't write letters but, nevertheless, Hermie felt he was in contact with him.

The biology was really going nowhere. He could not concentrate. His thoughts were like snowflakes, chasing each other to the ground, disappearing into its black surface just as soon as they hit. Julie was still an unknown quantity. He didn't know if she was a virgin. She could be one of those girls who fooled you, then turned out to be old-fashioned after all. She seemed too free for that, though. But she probably wasn't promiscuous either. He was getting a little crazy from all the heavy petting of the last few nights, which always led nowhere. Not that she pulled a freeze. It was just that the time didn't seem right, or something happened that turned them off, or the place was wrong. He knew it was as inevitable as New Year's, but it was easier to wait for New Year's.

Oscy had his problems but they were of a different nature. He was finding it hard to contend with Glenda's fierce appetite, and was looking for a way to cool it with her.

Hermie hadn't written home in a week. He knew he'd be getting a letter any day now. He ought to write to Ruth, too. His mother had told him, in her last letter, that she was pregnant, and very excited. Also, he supposed he ought to write to Mrs. Rothstein, or to Bernie himself, who'd just come back from service with two stumps instead of legs. He didn't know how to write that letter, so he was putting it off.

The biology text hit the deck. He was supposed to get something in for *The Nutmegger's* deadline, but hadn't the slightest idea what to write about. Maybe the elections. Dewey was hot on the campaign trail but he didn't have a chance. Roosevelt was a shoo-in. The University of Connecticut wasn't the most active campus in the world and Hermie thought nobody cared who won the election. He decided not to write about politics. He didn't know anything about politics anyway, only what he'd gleaned from his father's occasional outbursts for or against Roosevelt, depending on what the latest bulletin was from the White House.

Hermie'd read in some writer's manual that you should only write what you know, which tended to leave him without anything to write about. Then there was someone like Stephen Crane who wrote brilliantly about war and had never heard a shot fired. That was a contradiction right there. Noboby really knew what they were talking about, probably, but if you made some kind of name for yourself you could say anything and there'd be someone to quote you. Maybe he'd give up writing and become an accountant. At the moment it seemed to present less problems and far more security.

Then he tried to write a poem but it got too slushy when he started writing about love. Anyway, he couldn't, try as he might, find a rhyme for Julie. Except "coolie" and somehow he couldn't make a meaningful connection.

Finally he wrote a silly poem that never made it to the magazine, even though he was convinced it was an unrecognized masterpiece. Of course, the Editor was fraternity, so he probably wouldn't accept it on those grounds.

BEWARE OF GREEKS
by
Herman Green

It seemed like an eternity,
before I made Fraternity.
The first initiations were anything but smooth.
Each one seemed incredible.
The memory is indelible,
of crowding ten tall Pledges into one small phone-booth.
The Seniors seemed oblivious
Their pleasure was lascivious.

Their ever-ready paddles did anything but soothe.
   The ordeals all are finished now.
   The pain too has diminished now.
Maybe when I'm a Senior, I'll be tenderer to youthe.

He knew that "youth" didn't quite rhyme with
"soothe" and "booth" and "smooth," but thought that by
adding an 'e' he could soften it until it did, at least
visually.

Completely bored and unfulfilled by his evening's
"work," he tried to reach Julie, couldn't, so took himself
to see "Double Indemnity," which kept him thoroughly
satisfied until he was tired enough to call it a night. He
went to sleep thinking about Barbara Stanwyck. She
always played the bitch. He couldn't see why Fred Mac-
Murray was taken in by her.

26

Julie and Hermie were wrapped in each other's arms in her parked car on a quiet country road. Hermie was having terrible problems. The car was very small and there wasn't much operating space. If the doors and steering wheel could have been moved it would have been a considerable improvement. Hermie was getting very hot and bothered but it was frustration and pain rather than sexual excitement. Every time he thought he'd found a good angle, he'd hit his elbow on a door, or his knee on the gear shift. At one point he hit his nose so hard on the steering wheel that the tears came to his eyes. Poor Julie was being twisted like a rubber doll. So far she hadn't made any complaints. She was being very compliant with all his new arrangements. He'd had troubles with girls before, but they were usually of the "don't touch me there" variety. This was much more frustrating.

"Julie, Julie," he finally sighed, "why couldn't your father get you a Cadillac like all the other rich girls? A

guy'd have to be a dwarf to. . . ." He inadvertently hit
the horn with his elbow and startled them both out of a
couple of weeks' growth. "Jesus!" he yelled.

"How many rich girls've you known, Hermie?" she
asked. It was a joke.

He was in no mood for jokes. "None of your damn
business." He turned again and broke one of his precious
limbs on the door handle. Or that's what it felt like. With
a broken leg, a busted nose and a bruised elbow, he was
working up to a purple heart by the minute.

"Hermie," Julie purred, all sweetness and light. "Have
you ever heard those stories of guys dropping girls off in
the middle of nowhere?"

He looked at her warily, nursing his wounds.

"Well, sweetheart, here's a reversal." She suddenly
reached behind him and opened the door at his side. He
tumbled to the ground ignominiously, scarring for life
another part of his anatomy. He couldn't believe it as the
car rumbled away into the night, covering him with a fine
spray of country dust.

He sat there for a second, absolutely furious, but,
ironically enough, still terribly conscious of being all
swollen manhood. Maybe he was a secret masochist. He'd
read some of Oscy's plain-covered books about guys who
liked to do things with whips and chains. Although it got
him hot reading about it, he didn't quite see himself
wearing leather underwear, standing over some chained
female with a bullwhip. Though the way he felt about
Julie at this second, he couldn't be sure.

It was only a matter of seconds before the gleam of
headlights picked out his punctured silhouette in the night.
The car slowed down and a sorry Julie rolled down the
window and leaned out. "I'm sorry, Hermie. . . ."

He slitted his eyes and imagined her in chains at his
feet. Unh-uh, wouldn't work. She looked so edible that
he couldn't find any reproaches for her. He somehow or
other struggled to his feet and put his arms around her.

"Listen, Julie, this is stupid. I can't go back like I did last night. I can't and I won't, so forget it."

"I'm sorry, Hermie," she said again.

"I know you're sorry, but it doesn't change things. We've got to. . . ." He smothered her face with kisses and moaned in awful pain. "Something has to be done about our relationship," he said. He was afraid if he got any harder, the whole works might just drop off. He saw himself stumbling to the college doctor, holding the precious package in his arms. "Doctor, Doctor, please do me a favor," he sobbed.

"Now, now, young man, don't go to pieces."

"I just did, that's the trouble."

She looked at him, not knowing what to do, hoping he'd be able to come up with a solution.

"You know it as well as I do, don't you? Don't you?"

She nodded her head.

"It's not good for us. It's not." In anguish, "I *love* you."

She hugged back the only part of his body she could reach. The metal door panel formed an impenetrable barrier between them, even to Hermie's indomitable weapons.

"Julie, we've been saying that to each other for a *week*. A week! Seven days!"

"I know. I'm sorry." She opened the door and slid over to make room for him. He got into the car as well as he could, feeling almost like the men who'd been washed up on the beach at Normandy must've felt. He tried to take her in his arms, when suddenly a look of alarm crossed his face. Jesus Christ! There were just so many places a man could afford to be wounded before it was all over. This car just wasn't built for loving.

"Hermie what is it?" Julie asked anxiously, seeing the expression on his face.

He raised himself painfully from her. "Julie."

"What?"

"Jesus!" he twisted around, furious. "Iss diss not der gear shift? Ya, doss ist der gear shift!"

Julie giggled, amused. Dismayed, but amused.

"Iss diss not der auto horn?" He hit it a horrible blow. "Ya, doss ist der auto horn! Iss diss not der ashtray? Ya, doss ist der ashtray!" Totally frustrated, he blazed out, "Jesus Christ! Julie! Jee-zus Kee-ryste!"

Julie straightened herself out. "Maybe we better go back." She got out of the car on one side as he got out on the other. He moved to join her at her side. He took her gently in his arms and kissed her. His impulse was to pull her down right there on the grass. But it had been raining, and he feared the mud would provide even greater problems for them.

"I love you, Julie."

"I love you, Hermie."

He put his magnificent brain into gear. Somewhere there had to be a way. Dr. Herm the Magnificent turned on his Giant Thinking Machine. Someone who'd defeated the Armies of the Faithless and Waldo the Wizard could doubtless solve this problem in the flick of an eye. He began to pull out the seat cushions, rearranging them in his mind. Julie watched without saying anything. The whole thing had gotten a little ridiculous. Somewhere along the way spontaneity had been replaced by calcula-tion. She began nibbling on her nails.

"Hermie, my feet are cold, and I hope no one's watch-ing what's going on here."

Hermie sensed her feelings, and at the risk of repeating himself, said again, "I love you." She just nodded her head and shrugged. He replaced the seat cushions, trying to give them more space. If he did that, then they could . . . but in that case . . . on the other hand. . . . Ah-ha! He thought he had it! "All right, Julie. You have to do what I say."

She bit down on her lower lip.

"I want you to lie down."

She didn't move. He thought she was probably beginning to wonder if she even knew this strange creature, and what on earth was she doing with him out in the middle of nowhere. For all she knew he could be an escaped lunatic. God knows, he'd been behaving like one. She must be wondering what he was planning in his devious, madman's brain.

"In the car please, Julie. Please. I want you to lie down in the car. I love you, Julie, please."

"Well. . . ." She got into the car and lay on her back. She pulled herself across the car seat until her head was directly below the steering wheel. Part of her legs were hanging over the edge of the car seat, goose-fleshed in the October night. She looked 'like a patient etherized upon a table' under the x-ray machine that was the steering wheel. Hermie felt like the Mad Doctor of the movies.

Hermie was determined. He removed his belt and undid the buttons of his pants. He hated the crudeness of his attack, but it had to be. Victorianism went out with Victoria. Now everything was going to be George. The night air blasted at his swollen membrane. It was now or never.

Julie turned her head away, almost putting her eye out on a knob on the instrument panel. This was anything but romantic, nothing like he'd wanted it to be. She closed her eyes tightly. She looked as if she were awaiting a fate worse than death. Hermie lowered himself on to her.

"Julie," he said breathlessly.

She opened her eyes, looked up to kiss him and found a new and totally unexpected frustration. The steering wheel presented itself to be kissed, directly beneath his face and above hers. Since it held absolutely no sexual attraction for him, Hermie refused. To make oral contact with Julie, they'd've had to have had the tongues of lizards. Hermie saw her collapse. What had started out to be a romantic evening was turning out to be ludicrous, impossible.

"Look, Hermie," she ventured, uncertainly, "I think . . ."

Hermie would never surrender. "No, don't think." He propped himself up on an elbow and turned on the car radio. "Ahh, there's good news *tonight!*" Gabriel Heatter informed them. The next station he tried was bringing in a clear farm report. Next some great martial music, which would've been fine if he'd been named John Philip Sousa. He tried again and got the weather report, Gabriel Heatter, Edward R. Murrow in London after Dark, where Hermie thought he might have had more luck, and finally Bob Hope, funny, but not romantic. It was a losing battle. Winston Churchill was obviously talking out of a lack of experience. He could never have made that remark if he'd had to go through what Hermie was going through. Julie tried to sit up, but hit her head on the steering wheel.

"Hermie, you'll run down the battery."

Hermie felt himself getting angry. Oscy never told him it would be like this. "How about *my* battery?" He kept switching stations. "There's no more music in the world!" Finally he found a far distant, static-ridden version of "La Cumpasitra," probably all the way from Mexico City. That would have to do. "Julie," he whispered, "I wish it could be more romantic."

From beneath the steering wheel, Julie said, "Hermie, half of us is outside."

Hermie was in no condition to stop now. "It's okay. The good parts are inside."

She laughed, just a little, and relaxed. Somehow or other she managed to maneuver her head around the shank of the steering wheel. Hermie swooped down. His lips met hers. He felt her body rise to meet his in rekindled passion. It was going to be all right.

Until Hermie had a sudden, deadening thought. "Julie, are you, did you, I mean, will you?"

"Ssh," she said. "I am, I did, I won't."

"La Cumpasitra" bounced out into the night, passing, in its journey, two pairs of dangling legs, one pair practically strangled by a pair of grey flannel trousers. One light bleat of the horn sounded out over the music as if to make an announcement of its own, just as "La Cumpasitra" gave way to "Mairzy Doats."

27

An Indian summer hit town the next day. Hermie and Julie took a blanket and went out to the river to study. At least that was their ostensible intention. Julie lay face up on the blanket and dreamed out loud. "I'd like to be the first woman on the moon. I'd like to circle the earth in a Piper Cub with an Indian Rajah. I'd like to marry a millionaire and have twenty-five children, all angelic and redheaded, and a governess for each."

"I don't think your dreams are too unrealistic," said Hermie. "Most people have crazy dreams they're never likely to achieve. For instance, I'd like to be a reporter for a major newspaper, then I'd like to handle the city desk and retire at forty to write best selling books about my experiences." He traced the line of her profile with the tip of his finger. She had a beautiful profile. "I'd also like to place a kiss on the dimple in the left cheek of the most beautiful Julie I ever met."

"Hermie, you have to keep your dreams down to

earth," Julie laughed and presented the dimple on her left cheek to be kissed. Hermie accepted the challenge and was loathe to relinquish the downy softness of her cheek.

"Julie, have you ever been in love before?"

"No, yes, once . . . when I was six. He was eight and I liked him because he always wore torn sneakers. I was never allowed to wear torn sneakers."

"Rich daddy, right?"

"That's not a serious disease, Hermie. Honest, you can get over it."

"I know. I think you have. I didn't mean to throw it up to you." He kissed the dimple in her right cheek so it wouldn't feel neglected.

"Have you ever been in love, Hermie?"

Hermie didn't answer for a minute. She watched his face. "Once. I was fifteen. It was a thousand years ago." He didn't say any more. Julie didn't either.

They were silent for a moment. "Hermie, is the war going to end soon?"

"My father says it will this year."

"Do you think you'll go in the army?"

"I don't know. Maybe. If it lasts that long."

"You know, when I listen to the news and hear about all those people, children, old people, people like us, dying, losing limbs, losing their homes, sometimes I cry. The world sometimes is such a rotten place."

"I know. I think it always has been. I can't think of a time when there hasn't been a war somewhere."

"Not just wars . . . people to people. I guess it's human nature or something, but people just don't get along."

"I love you, Julie."

"I know, I love you, too. But it's easy for us. We're young. We don't have any responsibilities. It gets ugly after a while . . . love."

"It doesn't have to."

"My mother and my father hate each other. I think

they probably stayed together just for me. It's a good job there's money, 'course when she's in the south of France, he's in Rome, when there isn't a war on. They've had to stay put since the war . . . at least as close as opposite coasts."

"That's not us, Julie, that's them. It needn't be like that for us." Hermie brushed her cheek with his lips.

"I don't know anybody who's really, truly happy. Are you really, truly happy?"

"Right now? Yes. Not all the time, though."

"I think I'm the closest to happy I've ever been."

"Thank you," said Hermie.

She rolled over and looked up into his eyes. "Hermie, I have something very important to ask you."

"Sounds ominous. Shoot."

"Hermie, would you mind terribly if we changed our song from "Mairzy Doats" to something else?"

He pushed her down on the blanket. "Woman, you are hacking away at one of the institutions that have made America great. Just imagine if everyone wanted to change their songs. It'd be chaos!"

"But "Mairzy Doats" is so unromantic."

"Not really. It depends whom you hear it with. Anyway I like it."

"So we keep it, huh?"

"So we keep it. Julie, I've been thinking. There's not a soul around and you're so beautiful. . . ."

"I thought you'd never ask," Julie said happily, rolling into his arms. He ran his finger down her spine under her sweater. "Hermie, you have very educated fingers."

"Phi Beta Kappa," Hermie said, burying his lips in the warmth of the skin just above the belt of her skirt as he undid the zipper at the back.

28

Hermie arrived back at the fraternity house, happy and tired. He had the blanket over his arm and a load of uncracked books under his arm. As he opened the door he saw a line of boys, winding from the front door, up the stairs to the second floor landing, then up the stairs again to the third floor. The boys seemed to be stoic about what they were waiting for, quiet, patient. A couple were smoking. There was some quiet conversation. The only one who seemed at all nervous was Oscy, who was pacing the first floor landing like an usher at the Roxy during the Saturday matinee.

"Patience, brothers, patience," he was exhorting them. "All in good time. Just stay in line, please. Put out the cigar, Shellie. Where the hell do you think you are . . . in a pool room?"

Hermie looked a little dazed. The last time the frat house had seen so much action was during the initiations. He looked up to Oscy for an explanation.

Oscy saw Hermie come in, and ran down the stairs to meet him. "Hermie! I was beginning to think you wouldn't show!"

"Oscy, I live here, remember?"

"Ah, yes, of course."

When Oscy was playing the Impressario, Hermie knew it meant trouble. Oscy seemed altogether too nervous for this to be anything legitimate. After greeting Hermie he shouted to someone upstairs. "Hermie's here! Hold that place for him, please!"

"A logical question, if you please, Oscy. What is this?"

"It's Glenda!" Oscy announced, smiling broadly.

"Huh?"

"You wanted to meet Glenda, right? Well . . . meet Glenda." He gestured grandly toward the third landing.

"Oscy."

"She's a *hoo-er*, Hermie. That's why I didn't want to tell you. Took me a while to figure it out myself, but good old Glenda . . . she's a hoo-er."

"Oscy, what is she doing here?"

"Hermie, do I have news for you! A hoo-er is some-one who does it to anyone for . . ."

"Oscy, I know what a whore is. Just tell me what she's doing here?"

A door opened upstairs and Oscy rushed to the stairs. One of the frat brothers came down the stairs, shaking his hand vigorously from the wrist "Wow!" He started down the stairs to applause as the line moved forward.

Oscy rushed to the head of the line. "Hold it! Hold it!" he called out to the boy who was just about to enter the room. "Come on, Dave, get it up."

Dave smirked. "It *is* up."

"You know what I mean. Two bucks." Dave handed him the money. "Okay," Oscy said briskly, "Go on in. And no funny stuff. In and out, got it?" He slapped Dave on the ass, like a football coach sending in his first-string quarterback. "Move along." He started down the stairs, a circus barker manqué. "Have your money ready, lads. And fear not. There's enough for all."

One of the boys close to the head of the line started to look very nervous. It was Marty, who'd been pledged with Oscy and Hermie. Oscy patted him on the back. "Pull yourself together, Marty, you can do it." Marty smiled wanly and Oscy came back down to Hermie. "She's a goddamn gold mine, Hermie. I'm booking her into every fraternity house on Campus, if she lives." He laughed and nudged Hermie in the ribs.

Marty, unable to take the pressure, finally broke out of his place in line and stumbled down the stairs. The other boys hooted and booed as he passed.

"Don't worry about it, Marty," Oscy reassured him. "There's always tomorrow."

"Oscy . . ." Hermie began.

"And don't you worry, Hermie. Glenda's got a special rate for you. She's very anxious to meet you." He yelled up the stairs. "I still want that place up there reserved for Hermie! In front of you, Wallie!"

"I thought it was in back of me!" Wallie yelled down.

"Bullshit! In front!" He shook his head to Hermie. "There's always one guy."

"Oscy . . ." Hermie tried again.

"Yeah?"

"Glenda . . ."

"Yeah?"

"Is she . . . in our room?"

"Jesus, Hermie, I couldn't send her to a *stranger!*"

Hermie had been getting angrier by the minute. Now he was furious. He hadn't wanted to hit Oscy like he wanted to now since he was twelve, thirteen years old. His voice was a controlled scream. "Get her out of there!"

"What?"

"Get her out of that room!"

"Jesus, Hermie, she came special to see *you.*" Oscy

was all hurt feelings and pained disbelief, attitudes he'd perfected over years of practice.

"I'm going with Julie, remember?"

"What does that have to do with it? Every guy on the line is going with someone, except maybe Marty." He winked. "He's going with himself."

Hermie was fast approaching boiling point. "Oscy, you have one minute to get that . . . *girl* . . . out of my room!"

"It's my room, too, Hermie. Don't get so fuckin' possessive."

"One minute!"

Oscy changed his tack. "You don't know what you're doing, Hermie. I beg you . . . think about it. Look before you leap. We'll make eighty bucks right here. Eighty bucks! We give Glenda fifty and the other twenty we split."

Hermie gave him a questioning look.

Oscy answered quickly. "Ten dollars for linen!"

Hermie was about to answer, and in no uncertain terms, when the street door opened and some members of the faculty walked in. A couple of anticipatory egos and other pertinent parts were quickly deflated. The boys waiting on the stairs quickly dispersed, trying to look innocent, whistling and shuffling their feet in an effort to pretend nonchalant pursuit of their everyday routines.

Professor Otis looked grim. It had to be Professor Otis. He was about three hundred and ninety-three years old, according to the most recent census. His wife was equally antique. She wore rayon bloomers that hit just above the knee, and cotton stockings that hit just below. You could tell because she was so fat that when she sat down the adipose tissue of her thighs pushed her legs a good twelve inches apart. Her bosoms fell down below the belt of her dress. A couple of boys had once surmised that without clothes on she could probably have caused the Japanese Imperial Navy to surrender without a shot fired, since if that was what they were fighting for . . . forget it. The professor was the only one on the faculty who felt there was absolutely no reason why boys should be boys. There was too much in life that was important, for boys to be wasting the formative years of their lives in anything that didn't result in their knowing the gerund of "Vincere" or whether Henry VIII married Catherine Parr before or after Catherine Howard. He was definitely not the faculty member any of the boys wanted to see at that particular moment.

The other teachers with Professor Otis paled into insignificance at the side of this paragon of paragons. Later, not one boy could remember who the others even were. Professor Otis stood in silence for a thirty-second millenium, while the boys grew old and wore the 'bottoms of their trousers rolled'. Greybeards all, they wondered why sex had been such an important part of their distant youth. The smell of wintergreen pervaded the frat house as the ancient boys, now respectable pedagogues, creaked in their arthritic shells and waited for the axe to fall.

When his words finally came, they were almost anti-climactic. "Is there a woman up there?" Professor Otis demanded.

Oscy dredged up enough moisture to re-hydrate his tongue. "Professor Otis! Whatever gave you that idea?" he squeaked. In working on getting moisture back to his mouth, he'd overlooked the rehabilitation of his vocal chords.

Professor Otis' look was one of combined disbelief, disgust, distaste, revulsion, wrath, repulsion, repugnance, loathing and utter abomination. He was also scandalized. "We'll see," was all he said.

Oscy somehow recovered from his temporary paralysis and ran upstairs ahead of the professor. Paul Revere's mission was a piece of cake compared to Oscy's. He burst into the room on the third landing. Dave's protest

reverberated through the hitherto hallowed halls of Pi
Epsilon Tau. "Fuck you, Oscy!"

"My God!" Oscy called down from the bedroom door,
his voice reflecting disbelief, disgust, distaste, revulsion,
wrath, repulsion, repugnance, loathing and utter abomination. "There *is* a woman in there!

Professor and his retinue turned on their heels, a required talent for all men who yearn to become professors.

"The Dean's office. Now." That was all he said. They
left.

Oscy, his back against the wall, his blindfold still in
place, riddled by bullets, a last cigarette dangling from
his dying lips, collapsed slowly to the ground. "That's all
there is," he said. "There isn't any more."

29

Later in their room, Oscy began packing. Hermie sat on his bed, watching helplessly. There was no help he could offer.

"Narrow-minded, medieval, sons-of-bitches. They still think babies come from Macy's."

"Maybe if you hadn't kept insisting that Glenda was a nun."

"It was all I could think of."

"Why didn't you try sister?"

"She doesn't look anything like my sister."

"She doesn't look anything like a nun, either."

"I took a shot, Hermie, okay? I had to say *something*."

"You should've said she was invisible."

"I should have said she was invincible. Boy, what a wasted opportunity."

"You really brooding?"

"Aaah, who the hell cares anyway? Inside of a week

I'll be in the Army, fighting to preserve stupid institutions like this . . . with all due respect, Hermie, I'm very pleased to pack it all in."

"Wasn't that what you wanted all along, Oscy?"

"Oh, I suppose so, but I wanted an honorable discharge. I guess it's the Anglo-Saxon in me."

"Oscy, you've about as much Anglo-Saxon in you as the Amazon River has."

"Well, maybe it's that this way there's nothing for my mother to bronze."

"Do you think your father'll ever speak to you again?"

Oscy stuffed the contents of his bureau drawers into the already-bulging suitcase, dirty clothes mixed in with clean, books with socks for markers, one pair of pants that had socks, shoes, underwear and belt all attached to it, Oscy's nine o'clock class outfit. He'd tried a way of putting on a shirt in the same motion, but had given up, deciding that was a problem for the Time and Motion Study boys. "I think my father'll be all right. Secretly he's very proud. He admires business acumen. It's just that he gets overpowered by my mother. She'll have her job cut out thinking up a good story for the neighbors. Let's see, you're the writer."

"It's your story."

"Right. Okay, here goes. 'My Oscy! You wouldn't believe that boy. He wanted to complete his education. He has such a good head, what a future! But what a boy! I cry when I think about it. He said to me, 'Momma,' he said. That's what he calls me, Momma. 'Momma,' he said, 'I got to go. Boys my age are dying in defense of my country. I can't stand by and see the suffering any more. My conscience won't let me!' Ach, what a boy! 'Momma,' he said, tears in his eyes. 'Forgive me, but America needs me. My country calls. I have to answer.' Pretty good, huh?"

"Yeah, your mother has a strong streak of the dramatic."

"And where do you think she got it from?"

"Oscy, it usually works the other way round."

"Yeah, well I come from a screwy family."

"You can say that again."

"I come from a screwy family." Oscy looked round the room to see if he'd forgotten anything. Hermie threw him a sneaker that'd found its way under Hermie's bed. "Naw," said Oscy. "I'll leave that for you. Souvenir."

"Thanks a lot. It smells great."

"You're welcome. Do I have everything? I don't want to forget my freshman beanie and my song book." Oscy danced a jig in the empty half of the room. In the drawer of his nightstand he found some aging tangerines that his mother had sent and he'd forgotten to eat. He grabbed up the bag and was going to pitch it into the waste basket when he had an idea. He strode over to the open window.

Hermie, recognizing the gleam in his eyes, warned "No, Oscy!"

"What more can they do? Shave my head?" He started to aim his first tangerine, then stopped, a look on his face that made Hermie shiver. It was the look that preceded all of Oscy's most inspired projects. "I've got a better idea. Here, look after my stuff. I shall return!" Oscy took off from the room, the bag of tangerines clutched to his chest the way Sid Luckman might have clutched the pigskin. Hermie looked out of the window and watched Oscy burst through the frat house door and out onto the Green in a spurt of better broken-field running than he'd exhibited in any of the abortive college games. He ran straight to the Bell Tower. Hermie realized immediately what he was going to do.

"No!" he yelled from the window. "Don't do it, Oscy!"

Oscy paid no attention. He reached the Bell Tower, vaulted over the iron gate that was supposed to bar entrance, and began to climb the stairs to the top. Hermie covered his eyes and waited, dread in his limbs.

Suddenly the bell began tolling across the campus.

Concerned students and faculty, fearing a gas attack, or maybe invasion by the Japs, rushed out on to the Green and looked up at the Bell Tower. Oscy, omnipotent, was tolling the bell with all his might. On each stroke he threw down a tangerine from the top of the tower.

"There's one for the Dean!" he yelled triumphantly, hitting the poor old Dean splat on his hairless dome.

"And here's one for Otis, jolly old Otis." Splat! "And Goering!" Splat! "And there's one for Hitler!" Splat! "And Goebbels!" Splat! "And Himmler!" Splat! "And for Bernie Rothstein's legs!" The tangerines were flying faster, without aim. The students and faculty down below on the Green were clutching the walls, trying to stay out of the line of fire.

"And Paulie Marcus! And Mrs. Gary's son! And Hermie's sister's Al, and all the poor sons-of-bitches who flunked out of this rotten war!" He was yelling at the top of his lungs, the angry tears choking him as he threw down the rest of the tangerines. Like liquid orange anger, they hit the sidewalk and the Green, aimed in torment, squashed into debris. Oscy's bombs.

It was very quiet below. One of the custodians made a move to go stop Oscy. The Dean put a hand gently on the man's arm and shook his head. The custodian began to pick up the busted tangerines. People gradually drifted back to their rooms. An almost physical shiver ran through the empty quad.

Hermie swallowed painfully and blew his nose. He closed the window and put Oscy's bags tidily on the stripped bed. Oscy came in a few minutes later. He shrugged his shoulders. He looked on the point of collapse. He tried an imitation of the old Oscy. "Well, Hermie, the prodigal son is leaving . . . off to the battle, what?" His voice sounded as if the needle had been used on too many records.

Hermie held out his hand. "So long, Oscy."

"Think of me whenever you see any of our fighting

men in the newsreels. And . . . er . . . be good in school, will you?"

"I wish people would stop telling me to be good in school."

"Well, what I mean is, you're the last of the Terrible Trio, you know, first Benjie, now me."

"It's only temporary."

Oscy was fumbling for words. Sentiment wasn't one of his strong suits. "Anyway, we're depending on you because . . . you've a great mind." He picked up his bags and got as far as the door. "I'll drop you a line as soon as I know where I am." He turned back. "And Hermie, look in on Glenda, will you? I mean, soon as she gets out of jail."

"Okay."

"She's really a good kid, even if she is 32 years old. And . . . oh . . . say goodbye to Julie for me. Tell her I was called away quite suddenly . . . at the special request of the War Department. I like that girl, Hermie."

"Yeah, me too."

"Maybe I'll write to you in lemon juice, okay?"

"Good idea."

"Well, keep a light in the window, what?" He made his famous double-V sign and left. He leaned back into the room, smiled and waved, and was gone.

Hermie stood in the middle of the room. It seemed suddenly very, very empty. He and Oscy'd been together since kindergarten. In a couple of days Oscy'd be in uniform and he'd be . . . right here, good old Hermie, studying the Drama of the Middle Ages.

He could hear Oscy outside in the hallway, saying goodbye to some of the other boys. Oscy called out, "Marty? You in the bathroom?"

A muffled "Yeah," from the bathroom.

"Say one for me, kid."

"So long, Oscy. Give 'em hell."

It was quiet out in the hallway. Hermie heard the

thump, thump of Oscy's bags as he dragged them down
the stairs. As Oscy reached the bottom, he threw the
cases out onto the sidewalk. Hermie watched him from
the window. Oscy was silhouetted against the sky, part
of the Connecticut University skyline in the night-rose
sunset. With a characteristic final gesture, he raised both
arms and gave the old "fuck you" sign to the campus.

Hermie laughed to himself. "That's what's known as
an Oscy," he told the empty room.

30

Hermie bought Julie a hamburger before Study Hall. She was going to buy him a soda after Study Hall. It was a fair division of finances. Hermie was making more of an effort to study than Julie was. His life in the past few weeks had been so hectic with incidents, that the Big Brain was suffering a slight case of malnutrition. His vital organs had suffered an intense sea change. His liver was where his lungs should've been and his pancreas had changed seats with his sternum. His brain had somehow got completely mislaid in the mêlée. Initiations, love affairs, magazine reporting, Oscy-shines. It had been a very hectic couple of months. Being basically a serious person, he'd always put down the people who went to college for a good social life. Now, suddenly finding himself one of them, he felt it "behooved" him (Benjie-word) to get back to the primary purpose for his being here.

Julie, however, was suffering from none of his compunctions. She didn't feel like studying, and couldn't go too long without attention.

"You studying?" she asked, kicking him under the table.

"No, I'm only *trying* to study," he said, a shade sarcastically.

"What're you trying to study?"

Hermie gave up and banged his book shut. "I haven't the slightest idea."

Julie had slipped off her shoe. She ran her bobbysoxed toe up his shin, under his pants-leg. "How's your battery?" she asked.

"Running a little low, like my grades," said Hermie.

She poked her toe higher. "Wanna go for a drive, big boy?"

"If you don't cut it out, I'm gonna flunk this exam. I'm marginal as it is."

"You won't flunk any exam," she said kittenishly.

"Julie, it's serious."

"If that's all you're worried about . . . I can show you ways to pass exams you've never dreamed of."

Hermie looked at her, wide-eyed.

"Ah, I see you're interested."

"You mean . . . cheat?" In all areas except sexually, Hermie was a virgin. He was the one in the crowd who wouldn't steal from the dime-store. He was the kid who insisted on taking the wallet, stuffed with bills, that they found in the park, to the police station. He was the one whose face got red if the streetcar conductor forgot to punch his ticket. It wasn't that he was particularly pious. Those things just didn't occur to him. Maybe his mother'd been frightened by an electric chair when she was carrying him, or something. Anyone'd've thought that being in such close daily contact with Oscy would have changed all that, but strangely enough, Oscy'd respected his feelings, and when anything underhanded was going on, he usually left Hermie out of it. The time he took the bike

he was with David Katz, and when he made his weekly
foray to knock off the five and ten he usually took Benjie
for lookout, and Dottie Woizchek for cover. She had such
an innocent face. "The face of an angel!" the neighbors
said . . . "and the morals of a safe-cracker," they usually
added.

Hermie was surprised at Julie's suggestion. It seemed
to be out of character for her. She read his face. "My
dear Hermie, *everybody* cheats. How do you think General Eisenhower got through Andover?"

"Eisenhower went to West Point."

"You see! He managed to get through both! As to
Lincoln . . . God!"

"*Abraham* Lincoln?" Hermie asked, aghast.

"Of course Abraham. You know any other Lincolns?
Everybody knows he had all the answers in that big hat
of his."

"The answers to what, Julie?"

"Don't be so pedantic, Hermie. The answers to the
test questions, of course. And would you like to know
about Andrew Jackson?" She made it sound like a juicy
story.

"I'd really just like to study."

Julie ignored him. "For example . . . there's the one
where you slip all your crib notes inside your loafer. All
right, Hermie, I can see your question. The answer is yes,
you have to wear loafers. You slide your foot out of your
shoe, gaze down at your notes, then slide your foot back.
Repeat with other foot until passing mark is achieved.
Then there's the one where you write your crib notes on
a card that fits into the palm of your hand. The card is
tied to a string which goes up through the sleeve of your
slipover sweater, down across your chest, and is tied to
your belt. Yes, Hermie, you have to wear a long-sleeved
sweater. You refer to this index card for as long as it's
safe. Then, when the proctor gets suspicious, you kind of
raise your hand to scratch your head and, voila, the

index card scoots up your sleeve and is gone, as if by magic." She looked at Hermie to get his reaction. "Oh, Hermie, you've never cheated, have you?

"Nope."

"You know, I think that may be considered un-American. What's to become of you?"

"Very little," said Hermie.

"*Very* little?" she asked, cocking her head to give him the eye.

"Not quite so little," he admitted.

"Come on, let's go for a sexy drive. It'll be marvelous. I'm almost out of gas right *now*."

Hermie gathered up his books. "I've created a monster."

"Come on. Who wants to pass a miserable old exam anyway?"

"Certainly not *me*."

Julie took Hermie by the arm and led him out. "Let me tell you about Andrew Jackson. He had this little convertible, see? And the reason the girls all called him 'Old Hickory' was. . . ." The rest of the story was lost to the Study Hall teacher, who'd been dreaming about her own sailor off on the high seas.

It started to rain as they left the library. "I know a good place," said Julie. "No one'll be there in the rain."

Sure enough, the Quonset hut in the back of Gamma Upsilon was empty, save for its garden tools and a couple of sacks of fertilizer. Bedded down on a pile of empty sacks, Hermie forgot all his previous inhibitions about the place. It was a considerable improvement over Julie's car. The only disadvantage that Hermie could think of was the smell that permeated the hut from the sacks of fertilizer. Hermie found hidden depths in himself that night. It would always be a night to remember. And somehow, for years, he always connected the smell of fresh fertilizer with sex.

Coming back to the frat house late, Hermie was too

tired to do more than wave a lanquid hand to the boys lounging around as he passed through the common room. As he entered his room, he had the peculiar feeling that it was occupied. He looked around warily. Sitting on Oscy's bed was Marty, one of the ten Pledges. He jumped up nervously as he saw Hermie. "Oh, hi! I guess you're surprised to see *me* moved in," Marty said, hesitantly.

"Well, I knew somebody'd be moved in."

"They took a vote and you won me. Okay?"

"Okay." Hermie plopped on to his bed, supremely exhausted.

But Marty wanted to talk. "Truth of it is, they're sorry they pledged me."

"I'm sure that's not true, Marty."

"Oh, yes. They call me the Flying Dutchman of Pi Epsilon Tau."

"Take it easy, Marty. It's okay."

Marty's nerves were tangled like the inside of a golf ball. "If you want this bed . . ."

"No, this is my bed. That's your bed."

"What the hell you doing in this shitty fraternity, Hermie?"

Hermie was almost asleep. His efforts of the evening had done him in. "Huh?"

"Forget it. Whaddaya hear from Oscy?"

"Haven't heard anything. He's probably in the middle of Basic Training."

"That Oscy . . . he's gonna win every medal they got. Guys like Oscy always make the best soldiers." Marty was eaten up with envy. Oscy was what he'd always yearned to be. His confidence, his flare, his . . . there was another word. He remembered hearing it in lit class, but he'd forgotten it.

"Right," mumbled Hermie. He switched off his light and turned over, his face to the wall.

"You gonna sleep like that? Aren't you gonna take your clothes off?" Marty asked.

"They've been off," Hermie muttered from the approaches to sleep.

Marty sat up like a squirrel, excited, his ears a-twitter. "No kidding? You get laid?"

Hermie groaned, sorry he'd said anything. "No, I happen to be a nudist."

"Come on, Hermie." Marty plopped on to the foot of Hermie's bed and bounced up and down like a Christmas child. "Tell me."

"Well, Marty," Hermie *didn't* say, "What you do is you find the most beautiful girl in the world. If you're lucky you get to touch her skin and smell her hair. You can almost drown in the gold flecks in her eyes. Just hearing her voice on the phone can turn your whole body into an electric coil. The feel of her arms under your jacket, the length of her body pressed to yours. You see her from a distance, unexpectedly, and the perfection of her profile, the poetry of her form make her stand out from all the other people around, like a goddess, a beautiful golden Aphrodite. The curve of her hip, the most beautiful curve in the world, the roundness of her breasts, the nipples that harden and stand up when you touch them. The delicate downy line of her spine, her thighs, so warm and moist. You find and touch each secret part of her body with your fingers, your eyes, your lips. Your insides curl up and contract, your body becomes one huge, overwhelming desire. And when, inevitably, unbelievably, you're finally, totally together, there aren't any words to use. It's like climbing a mountain, or hitting a home run, or hearing Jascha Heifitz, but oh, so much better. Maybe it's like going to heaven. You want to laugh and cry. It's like poetry and music and ballet and all the art in the world."

"Well, Marty," he *did* say, "What you do is . . . you take off all your clothes and you play volley ball." He turned over, away from Marty and the light. "Will you go to sleep, please."

"That's all I do is sleep."

"Then go to the bathroom."

"Ha-ha. Very funny."

"Then go fuck yourself," Hermie dreamed he said.

After a while, when Marty saw that Hermie was fast asleep, he got up reluctantly, slung his towel around his neck and went out of the bedroom. He wished someone'd someday tell him something. If he died tonight, he'd never know.

31

Despite all Hermie's efforts to postpone them, the exams arrived 'on little cat-feet'. Like one of his worst nightmares he looked at the questions and found them to be in a language he'd never learned. He looked around the room and saw people he'd never seen before. The subject of the paper was one he'd never studied. All around him the Brains of the Western World were scribbling madly, on their way to immortality, as Hermie, out of place in this gathering of the great, found himself unable to put pen to paper. Even his name eluded him. Panic sat at his left elbow and Failure at his right. Fear crawled over the skin of his shoulders and trickled down his arms as Horror. The hands of the clock had picked up speed and were whizzing around in a frenzied race with each other. He found his eyes glued in fascinated horror to the second hand of the clock as it raced its way to eternity.

Hermie chewed on his pencil and sweated. He thought of all the years of his life that had led up to this moment of ignominious downfall. He saw his mother watching him as he played a part in a nursery school pageant. He saw her taking him by the hand to kindergarten, waving to him from the gate. He felt the dimes and nickels that his father had handed out for all the straight-A report cards he'd brought home. He saw the pride on his parents' faces as he'd graduated from grade school at the top of his class. He heard the tributes from his teachers. He saw the tears in his mother's eyes as she watched him going up for his high school diploma. "Oh, Mother," he thought, "What I'm going to do to you now!"

He began to chew on his finger nails as he looked around the room at all the other students, so complacent, so sure of themselves, so well-read, such incredible boors. He switched back from his nails to the pencil, then suddenly froze, as down the aisle, to his left, he saw a student had slipped off one of his loafers. Could he be?

He looked down the aisle to his right. Sure enough, another student, another loafer.

Two seats in front of him, he could hardly believe his eyes, yet one more student, one more loafer, one more pair of eyes gazing into a shoe.

Looking all around, like Peter Lorre on the Orient Express, letting his eyes do the work without moving his head, Hermie, very slowly, very gingerly, slipped a foot out of his own loafer. He looked down for the answer, like a bombardier sighting his target. He couldn't believe his eyes. Nothing there but a Thom McAn label. He suddenly remembered. And sure enough, slipping off the other shoe, there were his notes, neatly cut to fit into the heel of the loafer. Poor Hermie, a raw recruit in the ranks of the criminal, he'd misjudged his eyesight and the distance he'd be from his shoe. Probably subconsciously, not wanting to admit to being a *real* criminal, he'd written the notes so small that he couldn't read one word. He lowered his head, a millimeter at a time, so's not to be noticed. So involved was he in his deception that he didn't notice the proctor coming down the aisle, didn't even sense him standing there.

"Feeling ill?" asked the proctor.

Hermie, his head almost between his knees, feeling the handcuffs around his wrists, hearing the clang of cell doors reverberating around the prison walls, and the rattle of tin plates being banged against iron bars, did indeed feel ill, very ill, ill unto death.

He mumbled something. Somehow he managed to reserve enough presence of mind to slip his foot back into his shoe before the proctor could see his infinitesimally small notes.

"Want to take another exam on another day?" the proctor asked.

"No, I'm okay. It's just a . . . hot flash." Hermie couldn't think of anything else on the spur of the terrible moment.

The proctor, schooled in the ways of generations of students, was a bit suspicious, but not enough to take it further. "Well, see if you can 'hot flash' your way through this exam without falling over, all right?"

"Yes, sir," said Hermie, determining nevermore to err from the path of righteousness.

"For a good cause, wrongdoing is virtuous," a voice from Hermie's viscera spoke.

And from his conscience was answered, "What is left when honor is lost?"

The second time it was much easier. With conscience temporarily muzzled, after all, everybody did it, it was easier to prepare for all eventualities. Like the newcomer to sex who won't take any precautions preparatory to an evening out, because that would look like anticipation, Hermie had been reluctant about providing himself with adequate crib notes. Now, an old hand, his preparations

were more than adequate. They were elaborate. Talk
about contraception! In the palm of his left hand he held
a beautifully written crib card, clearly visible to the naked
eye from arm's length. Hermie had tried all different sizes
of printing until he'd hit the perfect one for the distance.
Not only that, he'd perfected the art of referring to it
without drawing any attention to himself. He'd spent much
longer on the card than he had on studying for the exam.

The proctor in charge either had a hangover or suffered
from night insomnia, because he was noticeably somnolent
at the front of the room and made little effort to sniff out
felons. One time, toward the end of the first hour, he
got up to stretch his arthritic old bones. As he dragged
himself down the aisles, an original ballet took place. It
could have been choreographed by Billy Rose. The
students wearing long-sleeved sweaters were legion. As the
proctor neared each of them, they raised their hands to
scratch their respective heads. In perfect balletic timing
the hands were raised and lowered, in rhythm with the
speed of the proctor's gait. Hermie was sixth in the
chorus line.

Exams all over, innocence lost, Hermie and Julie were
necking easily in Julie's car. It had taken time, but they'd
finally come up with a supremely workable set-up. Wit-
ness to the long way they'd traveled since that first terrible
evening, Hermie could even find the right kind of music
on the radio when he needed it. "As Time Goes By" was
playing quietly as Hermie nibbled at Julie's ear lobe. The
ear lobe felt cold, unresponsive. For some reason she
wasn't reacting as she usually did to his ministrations. He
sensed her heart wasn't in it. Finally, he asked. "What's
wrong?"

"Nothing."

Though still an innocent in many ways, Hermie knew
that when a girl said 'nothing', she meant exactly the
opposite. "Nothing, she says."

She tried to switch his attention away from her. "How'd you do in your exams?"

"I don't know how I did. I won't know for two weeks . . . and I told you that yesterday."

"Well, I thought . . . maybe you had an exam today."

"Julie, what's wrong?"

". . . Nothing."

"Julie, if I have to keep saying 'what's wrong' and you have to keep saying 'nothing' all night, we'll have to sit here until the war's over, and that's a waste of a perfectly good moon."

No response.

"Okay, let's play it another way. I accept your answer. Nothing's wrong." He tried to nibble again, with exactly the same dearth of results.

"Hermie . . ." tentatively, "I have a problem."

"If you tell me you're pregnant I don't know you."

"No," nervously. "I'm not pregnant . . . not to my knowledge."

"Then what's your problem?"

"Well . . . there's this boy I used to know and . . . he's in the Army. He's a corporal."

"That's very exciting."

"He's on furlough and . . . well . . . he's coming up to see me."

"When?" Hermie felt his jaw tightening. In the rearview mirror he looked the way his father had when he'd heard about the stock market crash. Hermie had only been a little boy, but he'd never forgotten his father's face.

"This weekend. I tried to tell him, but he would *not* take no for an answer."

"This weekend's the hayride."

"I know. And I tried to tell him . . ."

"Try again."

"Hermie . . . I can't go with you. Please try to understand. He doesn't mean anything to me. Really, it's strictly platonic."

"There's no such thing as a platonic relationship between a man and a woman."

"Well, this is. He's a boy from back home and I wrote
him letters because my mother made me *promise* to . . ."

"You mean you've been writing letters to another man
all the time we've . . . you've been . . . ?" Hermie was
grimjawed in his anger.

"He's in the service, Hermie."

"Bully for him."

"It'll only be for one night. He's coming up Saturday.
I can see you Friday and . . ."

"Who're you seeing Sunday?"

"Hermie, I think you're being very unreasonable."

"You do?"

"Yes, I do."

"Well, that's tough! I've been giving all my time to
you. I joined a fraternity for you. I'm sharing a room with
a nincompoop because of you. I'm cheating on exams
because of you. And I bought two tickets to a hayride
because of you . . . three bucks apiece!"

"You can return them."

"No."

"You can take someone else. I won't mind."

"That's very nice of you."

"Hermie, I can't go with you."

"You want to think over that last remark?"

"No. No, I don't. I've said it the best way I know
how. If you can't understand . . ."

Hermie took out his wallet and pulled out the hayride
tickets. "Here," he thrust them at her. "Never let it be
said that I don't do things for our boys in service. Have a
good time!"

He jumped out of the car and started walking away,
each step angrier than the last. He felt as if he were
walking directly into the fire of his own wrath. In a
minute he'd burst into roaring, blazing flames, consuming
the countryside and the car, and the disloyal bitch in it.

He kept on walking, each step a step away from the betrayal and into misery.

Angrily she banged on the horn. "You're a baby!" Julie screamed after him. "A baby!"

Hermie kept on walking, angry enough to kill. He heard the car start up behind him but didn't look around. He could hear it approaching, faster and faster. He still didn't turn. At the last moment, Julie swerved it around him and it roared past. A flutter of torn paper floated from the window, traveling at the speed of sound. It was the hayride tickets, torn to shreds. They floated down past him and joined the dust and exhaust that were all that was left of Julie.

Hermie kept on walking into the night as the sound of Julie's engine faded from his consciousness. After ten minutes of trudging, he realized he was tensed up into a tight knot of anger. His shoulders were hunched, his forehead corrugated, his hands balled into fists. He was so furious that when he even thought about Julie, he saw a bright red glare in front of his eyes. Just the idea of her petting in her car with somebody else . . . probably utilizing all his ingenious methods, too. He plotted twenty-five different mutilations for the guy, each one bloodier than the last. He worked out a nefarious scheme for waylaying him after he'd taken Julie home. Medieval tortures didn't come near to what was in store for that soldier boy. Then he began to make plans for Julie. Why should she get off scot-free? It was her idea. She could've said no if she'd wanted to. This was probably just her way of giving him the brush-off. God, she'd practically ruined his life, now she was blithely running off with some other jerk.

He started walking faster and faster, spurred on by his anger. Soon he was running. His feet pounded the dust of the country road, his arms pumped the blood to his heart. His eyes were narrowed into protective slits. He didn't see the road ahead, just followed his fury. Somewhere on the periphery of his vision he saw trees and houses going by. A cow passed him. He could feel his heart pounding, but he didn't tire. The longer he ran, the easier it became. Soon it was nothing but him and the white ribbon of the country road in the moonlight, an endless track taking him away from his misery. He knew he could run forever, away from everything, into a nothingness where there was no more feeling, no more hurt, no more love, no more war.

He'd heard about the exaltation of the deep. He was feeling drunk on the night air. It entered his lungs and seemed to purify them of all the anger and hurt he'd been feeling.

He ran until he and the road became one; he was the road.

He began to feel quieter in his mind, and realized he was slowing down. He still didn't feel tired, just exalted. It had been like an orgasm, building to its terrible, marvelous climax, then gently letting him back down, back into his own volition.

After his breathing slowed down, he realized that Oscy was probably right. The four-minute mile *was* just a state of mind. If the track coach had been timing him, he was sure he'd have clocked him at *five* miles in four minutes.

He walked the rest of the way home.

32

Saturday evening in the frat house. Someone had brought in some beer. There was a desultory group at the piano, forgetting the words to every song that'd ever been written. Hermie sat off in a corner, pretending to read a magazine. He wasn't even seeing the pictures on the page in front of him. It was useless. He started upstairs to his room. Maybe that's where the excitement was.

No one was in the room when he got there, which was just as well, because Hermie was in a singularly uncommunicative mood. He sat at his desk and read his memo pad, which made about as much sense as the magazine downstairs had. "Write to Aunt Mae. Call home Tuesday. Find out where Oscy is." "Answer Benjie's letter." None of it appealed to him. He went to the window and looked out, not seeing, into the night. He had nothing on his mind. Nothing was worth thinking about. There was nothing he wanted to do. Nowhere he wanted to go.

The door opened and Marty came in, apparently direct

from the bathroom, because he was wearing his towel like a flag. He had a copy of *Esquire* in his hand, which was even greater evidence that he'd just come from the bathroom. He acknowledged Hermie with a nod and plopped down on his bed to go through the magazine again.

"There's a picture in here . . . page 63. Wild!" He turned the magazine upside down and sideways, studying the picture. "I don't know, if they grow girls like that in Alabama, what the hell am I doing in Connecticut?"

"Playing with yourself," said Hermie. It was an automatic response. He hadn't meant to start anything.

"And I suppose you don't," said Marty.

"I don't have to."

"Ha-ha. Don't kid me, buster. You haven't seen your ever-loving in a week. Here, wanna borrow my *Esquire*? Page 63. Get yourself a good three-second thrill."

Marty was the kind of guy who irritated you whatever he said. Even when he wasn't saying anything he was irritating. You started out feeling sorry for him, because he wasn't popular, and pretty soon you realized he wasn't popular because he was unbearable, absolutely intolerable, under any circumstances. Hermie had been ignoring him as much as possible but they were sharing a room, so there had to be minimal communication.

Hermie, despite his mood, managed miraculously to contain his loathing of Marty. "Marty, this is the last room in this fraternity house that'll have you. So don't push your luck unless you want to move into the bathroom permanently."

"Ha-ha."

There was silence for a minute, then suddenly Marty remembered. "Oh, I forgot to tell you. A package arrived for you."

Hermie resisted a desire to throttle him. "Where is it?"

"Let's see. I think . . ." Marty was at his most obnoxious. "I think . . . oh, yes, I put it on the shelf there.

Miss Julie dropped it off . . . two days ago. Must've slipped my mind."

Hermie dived for the package on the shelf. "You are about an inch away from instant death. I hope you know that."

"Yeah. I like to live dangerously." Marty flicked through the pages of his *Esquire*.

God, how he hated Marty. He wanted to squash him with his foot like the bug he was, except he didn't think he could bear to look at what oozed out. Inside the package was a small cardboard box. And inside the box, his little bell. No note. Just the bell. He jingled the bell sadly and remembered 'With this bell I thee ring'. The bell sounded tinny, untuneful. He held it in his hand for a minute and leaned on his desk. It was all very final.

Marty interrupted his thoughts. "I trust it's bad news."

Hermie was on the verge of killing Marty with his bare hands. When the Judge asked him why he'd killed, he'd face the bench with an unwavering stare and say, "Because he was despicable," if he'd learned how to pronounce it by then.

"Listen, you creep." Hermie leaned over Marty threateningly. "I've been putting off telling you this, but you smell bad. For a guy who spends so much time in the bathroom, how about taking a shower every now and then?"

"I take showers."

"With soap?"

"Yeah, with soap. *Lux* soap, if you must ask. Like the movie stars use."

"Well, maybe you oughta try the kind Lassie uses." Hermie sniffed around Marty's side of the room. "What the hell . . .? That can't be you, Marty! What the hell is it?"

A funny look crossed Marty's face. Then he leaned over the side of his bed and peered underneath. "It's my laundry."

"Your *laundry*?"

Marty began to pull it out and gather it into a pillow-case. The smell was horrendous. "Yeah, with all I have to do around here, sometimes I forget to take it out. You guys, Jesus!"

"Two more days and that stuff could walk out of here."

"I'll take it out first thing in the morning. More I cannot do."

"You'll take it out tonight!" Hermie kicked the pile toward the door. "This stuff has trenchfoot!" He opened the door and shouted out into the corridor. "Somebody died in here! A year ago!"

Marty gathered his laundry up. He turned to Hermie pettishly. "You're nothing without Oscy. Nothing! And to get away from you he dropped out deliberately!"

Hermie shut the door on Marty, just missing his nose. "Out, Marty. Out. O-U-T. OUT!"

From outside the door, Marty yelled, "Well, I'm moving out, *too*. First thing in the morning."

Hermie yelled back. "I'll pay you to move out tonight!"

"For twenty-three cents you've got a deal."

The hall phone started ringing. Marty, even with his arms full of laundry, answered it. "Hello? Bellevue speaking. Who?" He dropped the receiver. "It's for you. I hope you're drafted!" He kicked on Hermie's door.

Hermie rushed out to attack Marty, but Marty managed to scuttle away out of danger, like a cockroach. Hermie picked up the receiver hopefully.

"Hallo? Yes." Not Julie. "This is he . . . hello? Yes, yes . . . yes, I'm here. Yes, I'll be home right away. Yes, I'm okay . . . and thank you for calling, Uncle Nat."

He stood in blankness for a couple of seconds, not hanging up the receiver.

A fraternity brother rushed up the stairs, panting. "That for me?"

"Huh?. . . . No." Hermie handed the receiver to the

other boy, who picked it up to hear a dial tone. Then he looked at Hermie's face.

"What is it?"

"My father died," said Hermie.

33

Hermie sat alone in the corner of the train compartment, looking out of the window but seeing nothing. He wasn't thinking about anything, just watching the pearls of moisture that his breath made on the window glass. Infinite tiny drops that spread a fog on the clear glass that faded at the edges until one single pearl ran down the pane and disappeared into the ancient wood and metal. He was still numb, anesthetized to acceptance of the awful news. There were other people in the compartment; a young couple, the man in uniform, a baby in her arms; a couple of businessmen en route for the City; an old couple, grizzled with lines, ancient, antiques in a modern world, but still very vital, very much alive. Hermie felt his eyes returning again and again to the old couple. They were both much older than his father . . . his dead father. He forced himself to think it. My father is dead. But it was still meaningless. His father would be there to meet him at the station. He always was. When Hermie came back from camp that time, his father had been there, the first person he'd seen on the platform, waving furiously so that Hermie wouldn't miss him. Hermie smiled. It was as if he'd been gone for a whole year that time he came back from the Adirondacks. As a matter of fact, he remembered, his parents had visited him only the Sunday before. He'd cried when he got down from the train, not because he'd had a bad time at camp, but because he was home and he'd just realized that for the first time in his life he'd been away from home. He hadn't thought about it at camp, where every moment had been crammed with activity. But the sight of his mother and father, so glad to see him, so incomplete, somehow, without him, had made him feel suddenly very sad.

His father'd been wearing his baggy work pants, and an old sweater that his mother kept trying to give away to the Salvation Army, but his father kept retrieving it from the sack. Hermie was glad his father wasn't all dressed up in his hairy suit. He liked him better in the old sweater. He'd be wearing it today, his pipe cold in his mouth, waiting for Hermie to come home.

But, of course, he wouldn't be there. He'd never be there again. Never. Never? You couldn't say that! Last time he'd seen his father he'd been just fine, standing at the door, waving goodbye to Oscy and Hermie in the taxicab that was taking them to college. You couldn't just remove someone from the picture like that. He suddenly remembered an old snapshot of him and his mother taken at Atlantic City when he was a baby. His mother had hated the picture of herself so much that she'd cut her own face out of it. It was pasted in the family album like that. It had always upset him to look at it.

It wasn't fair. His father'd been all right. He wasn't supposed to die. He hadn't done anything to anybody. He wasn't hurting anyone just sitting in his big chair, smoking his pipe and listening to Gabriel Heatter. Why couldn't he just've stayed there?

Oh, sure, everyone had to die. But why his dad? He hadn't even been ill. The only time Hermie remembered him being ill was one winter when he had a cold, and his mother put mustard plasters on everybody, just to be sure. His father had gotten better just as everyone else got ill, and he'd stayed off work so he could run up and down with hot tea and lemonade and aspirins. The only thing he could cook was scrambled eggs, so as soon as everyone was well enough to eat, he'd cooked them scrambled eggs, until the very thought of eggs made them lose their appetites.

Why were those old people sitting there across from him in the railway compartment and his father dead? They were probably mean old bastards who didn't deserve to live. That was always the way. Hermie felt himself getting angry. Something should've been done. They should've called him. Probably the doctor didn't even know what he was doing.

Dead was such a final word. What did it really mean? Hermie didn't know. No one in his family'd ever died before, at least not that he remembered. That was something that happened to other people, not to anyone you knew. There were things he wanted to say, things he wanted to know. He felt cheated. The door was locked now, and he didn't have a key. Once they'd gone to New Mexico, on a vacation. Hermie had wanted to buy a little cactus plant to bring back home. His mother kept saying, "We'll get it just before we leave." Then they'd left and were on the train before Hermie remembered they'd forgotten to get the cactus plant. It was too late then. They weren't any longer in cactus country.

He closed his eyes and stopped thinking. His head ached. This journey was never going to end. He hoped it never would.

Ruth met him at the station. Her body was blooming, all curves and early pregnancy. Her face was white and drawn. He held her for a moment. They didn't talk on the way to the house.

His mother greeted him at the door. She looked strained and tired, as if she hadn't been able to cry, which wasn't like her, because she could cry when someone didn't finish their breakfast cereal. Hermie held her in his arms and realized he was the stronger now. All those years when he'd been afraid of her discovering this, or finding out that. The times she'd forbidden him to go places or do things. That was all past. He'd made the jump and she accepted it, gratefully. The sudden shift in their relationship happened without words, in a second. Yet they both recognized it. She took his arm and led him into the house.

The relatives came. The clan had gathered as it had on so many other occasions, birthdays, Thanksgiving, graduations. Hermie remembered his graduation party. How noisy and happy it had been. The cheek-pinchings and the head-pattings. None of that today. He was greeted with a hand-shake, or a kiss on the cheek. Aunt Mae was the only one who broke into tears as he kissed her. His mother came over and sshhh'd her until she stopped shaking.

It was strange, the atmosphere in the house. Everyone wore somber faces, like unaccustomed clothes, and talked quietly, but it was almost as if it were impossible to keep that up for too long. The masks would crack and someone would laugh and others would join in. It wasn't disrespectful. It was necessary. Unrelieved gloom wasn't tenable. The grief was real but its tension was too unbearable. You'd forget it was a funeral gathering for a couple of minutes, then someone would remember, or maybe inadvertently mention his father, and suddenly it was real again. The only thing that bothered Hermie was that Ruth was sitting in his father's chair. No one should've been sitting there. But then he thought about Ruth's baby, not yet stirring in her belly, and decided that maybe she was exactly the one who should be there.

There was plenty of food, as there always was at his mother's gatherings. Neighbors had brought hot dishes and cold dishes and cakes and cookies and pies. The coffee pot was filled and re-filled. The whistling kettle boiled for tea, punctuating the somberness of the afternoon. Hermie circulated, shaking hands, receiving condolences. None of this had anything to do with his father. He could not feel grief. He wasn't hungry. Someone kept filling his coffee cup, and he kept drinking it. Most people kept their voices low. It wasn't necessary, thought Hermie. His father wouldn't wake up. They didn't have to keep quiet. But he found himself talking in the same quiet tones.

His mother sat on her chair, half-listening to the talk going on around her. She had a handkerchief tucked in the bosom of her dress, but the only time Hermie saw her use it was when she spilled a spot of coffee on her lap. Her grief wasn't something she wanted to put on display. She'd always been a very emotional woman, never hesitating to laugh or cry, or scream in terror at some awful accident that almost happened. But Hermie thought he understood this was different. This she had to keep to herself.

The afternoon turned dusky, images passing in front of Hermie in an atmosphere that seemed to have been created out of unreality. These people weren't gathered together because of his father's death. It was a mutual fear and dread of their own mortality that had drawn them together. You couldn't mourn for a man who was dead, only for yourself because you were suddenly alone. Hermie had a silly feeling that his father should have been there. In his quiet, accepting kind of way he'd have understood all this.

The thing that hit Hermie with the greatest impact was that he didn't feel fourteen any more. His father's death had made the transformation. He felt as if he were the oldest person in the whole room.

After a while, Hermie went up to his room and sat at his desk. All around were reminders of his childhood. The last time he'd sat here was just before he took off for college. He'd felt then that this would never be home again, and now he was sure. His father would never bang on his door and tell him to turn down the phonograph. His mother wouldn't stand, arms akimbo at the door and express horror that anyone, let alone a son of hers, could live in such a pigsty. No more of those awkward confrontations when his mother had persuaded his father that it was his job to talk to Hermie. His father had dutifully come up and tapped on the door, but they usually ended up playing chess, which Hermie let his father win.

There was a tap on the door and Ruth came in. She and Hermie had never been close, but he felt a great stirring of affection for her now. She'd been a mainstay downstairs, substituting for her mother, with whom she'd had so many bitter arguments. But none of that meant anything now.

She collapsed into Hermie's armchair and sighed, rubbing her eyes. "Do you have a cigarette?"

Hermie threw her his pack.

"Every time I tried to take one downstairs, everyone made remarks about it not being good for 'little mother' . . . all that stuff. I'm having a nicotine fit."

Hermie nodded. Other people always liked to run your life for you.

"Everybody's gone. Except Mrs. Bates. She's cleaning up in the kitchen, you know her. And Aunt Mae and Aunt Tess, they're with Mom. But everyone else is gone. Well, that's that . . . it was a nice service." There was silence for a few minutes as she puffed on the cigarette.

"Hermie, I think I know what's in your mind. You . . . want to leave school. Join the army."

He shrugged his shoulders.

She went on. "That would be like running away. Really it would."

He looked at her, wondering how she knew so much about him. They'd never talked to each other.

"You're smarter than me," she said. It was something she'd accepted a long time before. "It's okay. I'm older, but you're smarter. You're the one everybody's counting on. But it's okay. I've got Al and . . . and the baby. We've all got Mom and . . . some responsibilities we didn't have two days ago."

"How the hell can I go back to school?"

"Dad saw to it, he had some kind of policy. The money's there. You may want to work a little for some . . . side money, if you want to, but . . . the tuition's all there."

Hermie didn't say anything. His eyes felt tired and his head ached.

"You didn't know he had a heart condition. Neither did I. They both felt we didn't have to know . . . like if we didn't know it couldn't happen. Right?"

He nodded, still not saying anything.

"Hermie, Al is in service. The family's got one blue star in the window. For the time being one's enough." Her voice broke for the first time. Hermie turned away. He hadn't been thinking of her as a woman whose husband was away in the service. He'd been thinking of her as Ruthie, his distant sister with the big tits, whom he'd never had much to do with.

He rubbed his hands over his face, stretching the eye creases, pulling the skin taut across his cheeks. "I'll have to go sometime."

"Maybe not. Maybe it'll be over. Meantime, Mom doesn't need to worry about *you* being in the Army."

"Why didn't they tell us?"

"I don't know. I don't think it would've changed

anything. You know how they were . . . 'don't tell the children'. We'll always be 'the children'. That's the way it is."

"I might have acted differently."

"You acted fine. You're golden. You could never do anything wrong as far as they were concerned. Hermie, I don't want to move into things that don't . . . that are Mom's, but promise you'll go back to school, okay?"

"I have to think about it. It has to be up to me." Where had he heard those words before? A million light years ago in his youth, in Dubrow's with his father after graduation.

"Maybe next time it can be up to you. This time, one more time, Hermie . . . it's up to Dad. It's what he wanted."

Hermie was wrong again. It still wasn't up to him.

Ruth stood up and straightened out her skirt at the back. "Uncle Nat said he'd go through Dad's things with you, but Mom thought maybe you'd rather do it by yourself. I'm taking Mom over to my place for the night. If you don't want to stay here, there's room for you."

Hermie shook his head.

"Well, that's up to you." Finally, something was up to him. "We'll see you in the morning, okay?" He nodded. "Oh, there's stuff for breakfast. Rice Krispies, Wheaties . . . whatever you like. And there're some bananas. Well, see you tomorrow."

Hermie was alone. He heard footsteps and doors opening and closing. A car door. Then he was alone.

He sat for a few minutes, then wandered into his parents' bedroom. It'd always been a room of great mystery to Hermie. As a little boy he'd crept in for comfort after a bad dream. Later, when he was nine or ten and just finding out about sex, he'd spent hours peeking through the keyhole, trying to catch a glimpse of something, anything. When he brought in the Sunday paper, he'd nonchalantly try to check out the positions of the bodies under the blankets. Were they doing anything to each other? Were they close enough to be touching? He'd try to check out whether his mother was wearing a night-gown, but he never did find out, she was always so deep under the covers. Anyway, she didn't look much like the girls in the illicit *Esquires* that Oscy sometimes got hold of, so he didn't suppose his father was interested in her sexually. Then at eleven, when Oscy told him the *real* facts of life, he knew *his* parents would never do anything like that. It was just out of the question. He'd had an awful fight with Oscy when Oscy asked him how he thought *he* got here if they hadn't done *that*. Hermie was furious at the suggestion and was sure Oscy had his facts wrong.

After that he didn't take such a morbid interest in his folks' room. It was just a place where they slept. But he never could get over the feeling that the chest of drawers contained secret things that were not for a boy to know about. It was just another room in the house, but implicitly out-of-bounds. Not a room to plop down with friends or lie on the bed and listen to records. It was their place, closed off to him.

The room was serene now, nothing going on. Just a bedroom in somebody's house. It was slightly stuffy. The drapes had been drawn, probably since his father had died. The bed was made, a fluffy chenille coverlet care-fully draped the same depth at each side of the bed. There were two night stands. On one of them his father's spec-tacles were still sitting. Hermie closed his eyes and pushed them into the drawer. There were photographs of Hermie and Ruthie on the bureau. Ruthie was in the bridesmaid's dress she'd worn for Cousin Rose's wedding. Hermie was in a suit, posed for some formal occasion or other, looking very proud and self-conscious.

In the closet his father's suits, shirts, ties, belts, a couple pair of shoes, the suits neatly hung, the shoes highly polished. What did you do with a dead man's suits?

His father's desk had been left untouched. There were

bills in two piles, paid and unpaid. A couple of memos
on the calendar: "Dr. Rosenthal 2:00 Friday" and
"Check with Bernie," and "Roofing man." A small black
book held his father's telephone numbers. Hermie
thumbed through it. It was scarcely the traditional little
black book. He laughed, despite himself. Doctors, Insur-
ance Agents, Partner, Aunt Mae, and the latest entry, in
capital letters "HERMIE'S NO. AT COLLEGE." Followed by Mrs. Gilhuly's number, carefully printed so
there could be no error. Then there was a line through
that, and underneath was written: "HERMIE'S *NEW*
No. AT COLLEGE," followed by the frat house number.
He'd never really thought about it before, in just those
terms, but he was one of the most important people in
his father's life. And he'd never done anything about it.
Now it was too late. They weren't in cactus country any
more.

He cried for the first time. He'd spent a whole life,
eighteen years, thinking about himself, never once about
his father. And now his father was dead and he couldn't
tell him. Why hadn't he done more when he'd had a
chance? He'd never told his father he loved him.

He found a bottle in the kitchen cupboard. He didn't
know what it was, but he drank it anyway.

He went back to his father's desk and painstakingly
began to reconstruct a life he knew nothing about. There
were old, yellowed snapshots of his father and mother
when they were young. In bathing suits, on the beach, in
an open touring car. So young. They couldn't have been
much older than Hermie.

Cufflinks, tie pins, collar stays. Some Track Medals . . .
"100 yd. dash 1921 – Second Place" . . . well, that gave
him one up on his son. A photo of his father as a boxer.
A boxer?

Then, in a separate package, a whole bunch of Army
stuff. Discharge papers 1918. Regimental insignia. A
Second Lieutenant's bars. Some medals and ribbons. More

photographs. His father as a doughboy, as an officer. Some letters from France. Is it possible his father had had the same kind of doubts about life as Hermie? He'd probably had the same kind of decision to make. Well, he'd obviously made it. He'd gone in the Army first. Maybe that's why he wanted Hermie to go to college first. Perhaps he'd wanted his son's life to work out as he'd've liked his own to work out. Wow, that was a killing thought! He wanted me to be him at eighteen, but doing it differently. He felt very close to his father at that moment.

A pair of baby shoes. God! They must have been Ruth's. Tax forms, bank books, post cards, pills, all colors and sizes.

The desk could almost have belonged to a stranger. Hermie wondered why he hadn't known anything about this man. Hadn't he ever asked? Hadn't he ever cared? There was a whole life in those drawers that Hermie knew absolutely nothing about. It was scary. His father had always been the quiet one in the family, kind of swamped by his mother. Hermie wondered if he'd ever thought about the man he'd been, about the past, or had he just put it behind him and gone on. It'd been hard for them during the depression. Two kids and a mortgage. It couldn't have been easy. Maybe he'd just decided to forget the old Simon and be the Simon everyone had come to expect him to be.

Maybe that's what we all become, what people expect us to be. It was a horrifying thought, but Hermie felt he was probably closer to the truth than he'd ever been in his life.

In the long run it probably never was up to you.

He sat at the desk until it got dark, thinking about his father, thinking about himself.

34

He woke from his thoughts suddenly, aware that somebody was in the room. His heart stopped for a second. He quickly switched on the light. My God! Oscy! In uniform, looking tidier than usual, his hair cut cruelly short.

"I saw your mother and sister. They said I could come up. I'm very sorry, Hermie. Your father was a nice guy. . . ." Oscy was ill at ease. It was an unaccustomed role for him.

Hermie was just staring at him.

"Yeah, it's me."

"You didn't write one letter to me. Not one."

"There's always a reason, Hermie."

"Oh, sure."

"I was ashamed." He sighed and explained, painfully. "I'm stationed at Governor's Island. Governor's Island, Hermie . . . right in the middle of the Hudson River. Can you believe that? Me, a born combat soldier, stationed at Governor's fucking Island! I come home four nights a week . . . in the dark."

"What do you do?"

"I don't know if you're ready for this. I'm a Clerk-typist. You like that? A Clerk-Typist with Oak-leaf cluster. A Clerk-Typist, with my figure! Stupid Army idiots, they were impressed with my college background. I tried to tell them I ran a hoo-er house, hoping they'd see I was officer material. But no . . . they said I'd have to be a Clerk-Typist. I can't type five words a minute and three of those are misspelled. Christ, the enemy has to be awfully stupid to be losing a war to the U.S. Army. Well, anyway, we all have to do our part. 'They also serve who only sit and type'. How's it going?"

"I've been going through my father's things."

"Yeah."

"It's funny . . . a whole life took place here, and I didn't know anything about it. It was going on . . . and it ended . . . and I didn't notice."

Oscy felt uncomfortable. He was at ease when he could make jokes. There weren't any jokes here. "Yeah," was all he said.

"It's weird. He came home, sat down at the table. Smiled at my mother . . . and died." Hermie paused. "He was only forty-three years old. I don't think that's very old."

"He was a nice guy." Oscy looked around uneasily. "You all alone here?"

"There's some Rice Krispies." They both laughed. "And a banana." Oscy laughed. Hermie didn't. "It's weird. I mean, there's a war on. Guys are getting killed. Who expects his father to die of a heart attack?"

"I don't know."

"It's weird."

"What happens now?"

"I'll stay for a few days, then . . . they want me to go back to school."

"You should. You could end up on Governor's Island. Take my word for it, Hermie. You're better off in that crummy school than you are in the crummy Army."

"I'll probably . . . at least finish the semester." There! It seemed he'd made his decision after all.

"A wise move. That's what I'd do if I were in school."

"I looked up Glenda, like you asked me to."

"How is she?"

"I couldn't find her."

"Did you try the bakery?"

"Yeah. She must've left town . . . on a rail."

"Well, no sense in her staying around where she wasn't appreciated. God, we could've made a fortune. Bet she's part of the War Effort. That should help us win."

"Did you know my father won some medals in World War I?"

"Really? I guess he never talked about it, huh?"

"Never."

Oscy couldn't take too much of this. He was getting twitchy. "Hermie? How long you going to do this?"

"Do what?"

"Mope? I don't want to be disrespectful, old top, but you're gonna have to shape up sooner or later."

"Yeah. What do you suggest?"

"Your father was a good guy . . . and a *man*. And I think he'd appreciate it if his son went out and hoisted a few in his memory."

Hermie considered it.

"Because I'm in uniform, I can get into any bar. Your father was a goddamned combat soldier, Hermie. Let's go out and hoist a few to his fond memory."

Hermie thought for a moment, then finally said, "You're on!" He stuffed the medals and papers back into the desk drawer.

"Attaboy!"

"We'll take *his* car!"

"He'd love it," cried Oscy.

35

It was a nondescript bar. Just a bar. And crowded, like every other bar and hotel and restaurant in this crazy war. Everyone was always going off somewhere, or coming back from somewhere. The barkeepers must've been raking it in. For them the war was one long celebration, with the cash registers jingling like the Old Bells of Bow. It was a good job Prohibition was over.

Oscy and Hermie found a corner for themselves and solidly set themselves in for a long night of drinking. Neither of them was really what you'd call drunk. Hermie was getting progressively more melancholy, which hadn't been the idea at all. Oscy was slowly drinking himself into a scene from "Dawn Patrol," where the survivors of each mission drink to their fallen comrades.

"You know what kills me?" Hermie asked, not addressing anyone, so not expecting an answer. "We never talked. Nobody in my family . . . we never talk. I mean, I wanted to, and I thought about it, but then it was too late to do anything about it. I mean, when you never get into the habit, it's easy to get out of it. Oh, chit-chat, gossip, every day come-and-go kind of stuff. But nothing that was important. Nothing you'd want to report for posterity. I guess basically I come from a long line of non-talkers."

"Yeah, well, we're not exactly the last of the great conversationalists, either."

"But you know those families, like the Vanderbilts and the Rothschilds, and those English types, like the Sitwells, I mean, you could probably have recorded their whole goddamned dinner conversation, if they'd had records in those days, and made a play out of it."

"Well, let's face it, Hermie. The Greens and the Bergs are scarcely literary aristocracy. Oh, what the hell! Who cares? Here's to your old man." He raised his glass.

Hermie did the same. "To my old man!"

They downed their beers, then Oscy, to Hermie's horror, took off and hurled his glass against the wall, where it shattered into a dozen flying pieces.

"What the hell you do that for?" asked Hermie.

"That's the way it's done, boy."

The bartender stumped over threateningly, his one good eye focused on Oscy. Oscy forestalled him, stole his thunder. "How much for the crystal, my good sir?"

"A buck," the bartender said grudgingly.

Oscy pushed a dollar at him. "Here, keep the change." Magnanimity became the new Oscar.

"This *is* a buck," the bartender said, turning it over to make sure.

"Win a few, lose a few," Oscy tossed over his shoulder as they both left the bar, laughing.

In the second bar, the clientele was much the same. Except for the nude over the bar, and the fact that this bartender didn't have a glass eye, it could've been the same. There was the same crowded mixture of uniforms and civilians, all celebrating the fact that they were alive.

Oscy and Hermie had been drinking steadily, one beer at a time, nothing flamboyant. Their drunk was building nicely. It had a good stable foundation. It was a warm drunk, a friendly drunk.

". . . just wasn't the same when you left, Oscy. Something went out of my life. A light went out."

"Life goes on," said Oscy, philosophic, philoso . . . beerily.

"If it wasn't for Julie I'd have gone off my rocker."

"Ah, Julie, the pearl of the South."

"She's not from the South."

"It's a figure of speech, schmuck."

"She happens to be from New Haven."

"Well, you can't say Pearl of New Haven."

"Why can't you say Pearl of New Haven?"

"How do you know she even came from New Haven?"

"Because I said she came from New Haven."

"I only have your word on that."

"I can prove she came from New Haven."

"Prove it."

"She *told* me she came from New Haven."

"You could be lying."

"Why would I lie about New Haven?"

"I don't know. I'm sure you have your reasons."

"Schenectady. I'd lie about Schenectady, but not about New Haven."

"Would you lie about Altoona?"

"Altoona? Yes, dammit, I'd lie about Altoona."

"Then you'd lie about New Haven."

"Yes, I probably would. Come to think of it, I might lie about New Haven. But Julie wouldn't lie about New Haven. She's a good man, Julie."

"One more toast!" Oscy raised his glass. "To your old man!"

Hermie raised his glass. "To your old man!"

Oscy shook his head. "No, to *your* old man!"

Hermie agreed. "Right. To *your* old man!"

Oscy threw his arm around Hermie. "Hermie, you're all right in my book." He lifted his arm as if to throw his glass.

Hermie stopped him. "Here, allow *me*." He tossed his glass against the wall. Oscy followed suit, then pulled out a dollar as the bartender descended on them. He leaned over and whispered at the bartender, "Win a few, lose a few." Then he and Hermie laughed and helped each other out of the bar.

In the next bar everything had been done over in red plush. Otherwise it resembled the other bars in the boys' odyssey that night.

Hermie confided in Oscy. "Everyone in my family, they're all expecting great things from me."

"They should. You're a fuckin' prince."

"You too."

"Thank you."

"I mean it. You expect a lot of me, too, don't you?"

"We all do. Everybody does. You're a fantastic man and a credit to your race."

"Only one who never expected anything of me was Julie."

"That's 'cause she's a hoo-er."

"You're thinking of Glenda."

"Constantly." Oscy drained his glass and ordered two more.

"Julie let me be whatever I am."

"And what's that?"

"I don't know. She never told me." He had a sudden thought. "And now she never will tell me."

Oscy thought that was funny, so they both started laughing and collapsed into each other's arms, simultaneously throwing their glasses at opposite walls. Crash! !

A group of soldiers were sitting off in a corner, drinking quietly. They looked older than Oscy and Hermie. Some of them weren't wild about the intrusion of the two,

obviously plastered boys. Oscy stood over the group, and
as if he were reading from a clipboard, barked out, "All
right, you guys! When your name is called get in the
truck! Franconi, O'Reilly, Wesoloski, Goldberg, Sheiner,
Ramrus, Gross, Swenson, Ramirez, Patty, Laverne and
Maxine."

The soldiers laughed. The kids were harmless. Then
one of the older ones, seeing Hermie in civvies, play-
fully plopped his cap on Hermie's head. It wasn't a very
good fit and slid down the bridge of his nose, obscuring his
vision. "There you are, sonny," said the older man. "Now
you're a big boy."

Everybody laughed, but Oscy kept his eye on Hermie.
He'd always been unpredictable, and even though he
was drunk, Oscy knew he could be touchy as hell. Hermie took the hat and flung it the length of the bar. The
hat hit the wall, where the beer glass had so recently
shattered. The soldier lost his laugh. He was about to say
something when Hermie uncorked a weighted right hand
shot to the jaw of the older man. That shot had behind
it all of Hermie's worries and doubts, all the challenges
he'd given himself, his pent-up frustration, the death of
his father, having to go back to school, his anger at all
the people who were molding him into what they wanted
him to be, Julie's betrayal, Benjie in the Marines, Paulie
Marcus gone, orange layer cake and Oscy in the bell-
tower aiming tangerines. The soldier, taken unawares, was
knocked ass-over-backwards by the force of Hermie's
shot.

The others came to his rescue, and pretty soon it was
a quality brawl, the soldiers against Hermie and Oscy,
who had no choice but to side with his pal.

Some sailors from another group across the room
decided to get theirs off against the Army, and it was a
wonderful fight. Not a table was left standing, not a glass
unbroken. The bartender, who had wild west pretensions

when he was younger, stood up on the bar and cheered them on. He hadn't seen anything better since the last Gary Cooper western at the Kingsway.

36

Since all good things had to come to an end, Hermie and Oscy soon found themselves driving home, somewhat the worse for wear. Hermie had some painful bruises and a rapidly-closing black eye. Oscy had some superior welts, but mostly he was just drunk.

Hermie drove very slowly, because the streets were moving very fast and he had to concentrate. His depth perception was all shot to hell, so was his breadth perception and his heighth perception, so that obstacles that loomed up in front of him had no easily perceived width, height or depth, and he was forced into elaborate maneuvers to avoid being trampled by buildings and stores. As he began to get the hang of it, he said to Oscy, "If those guys are all we've got going for this country, we're in a lot of trouble."

From his twilight consciousness, Oscy fuzzed into semi-wakefulness. "Hmmmm? Haaah?"

"Good with artillery, but when it comes to hand-to-hand . . . nothing," said Hermie.

"You referring to our late fight?"

"Yeah, some fight."

"I hate to break the news to you, Tiger, but you were knocked on your ass five times."

"Oscy, I got up, didn't I?"

"Four times."

"Bullshit!"

"Right, that's exactly what it looked like to me."

"I'm joining the Navy."

"Yeah, make it the Spanish Armada."

"I got up five times, Oscy, you can't count and you can't drive, either." Hermie squinted over the steering wheel. "Slow down, you jerk. You're gonna hit somebody."

Hermie had convinced him he was at the wheel. "Oh, sorry," Oscy apologized.

"I can't make out these signs. Which way is Altoona?"

"Precisely," said Oscy.

"If you don't slow down, Oscy."

Oscy straightened up and stared straight ahead. "How's that?"

"Better."

"I like this car, Hermie. Handles real easy. You scarcely know you're driving."

"I may *marry* Glenda, you know," Hermie confided.

"You should. She's a good lay." Oscy approved. "And a gold mine."

The car began to slow down.

"What are you slowing down for?" asked Hermie.

"Maybe we're there," said Oscy.

"You've been driving on an empty gas tank."

"Not easy," said Oscy, shaking his head, and continuing to shake it because he couldn't remember how to stop.

"Where the hell are we?" asked Hermie.

Oscy smeared the misty side-window. "Looks like Ireland. My mother came from Ireland. The hard way."

"Pull over to the side," said Hermie, "I think you're drunk."

"Check," said Oscy smartly. He opened his door and fell out on to the sidewalk.

"We better ask somebody." Hermie looked across at where Oscy had been and suddenly wasn't. "Oscy?" He looked in the glove compartment. "Oscy, you're not funny." Then he had an afterthought, opened up the glove compartment again and yelled in, "You never were funny."

Hermie got out of the car and walked around it to where Oscy was sitting, propped up against the door. Hermie made one of his split second judgments, for which he later became famous. "You're in no condition to drive."

"Don't be silly," Oscy said. "Hop in." He toppled over onto the sidewalk.

Hermie helped him to his feet. They began to stagger up the street, leaning on each other. They stopped and Hermie wet his finger and held it up to the wind. Satisfied, they moved on.

By a devious route, and protected by the fates that look after drunks and little children, they somehow arrived at Hermie's house. It was very late. The house was dark, except for one bulb crazily swinging in the hallway. Or maybe it was Oscy and Hermie crazily swinging in the hallway. They were clinging to each other. Hermie began helping Oscy up the stairs.

"Come on, Hermie boy, you can make it," said Hermie to Oscy.

"Oscy, you are the salt of the earth and a true combat soldier," said Oscy. "What the hell you doing on Government Ireland?"

"I don't know. Maybe they needed me to subdue the typists. But I'll get off, I'll get off," Hermie assured him.

"Should make you a General." He shouted up the stairs. "A General! A fuckin' General!"

"Sshhh, not so loud, Hermie. You'll wake up your family."

"Nobody's home, jerk," Oscy reminded him.

" 'Course there is," said Hermie, "There's always somebody home."

"Naaah," said Oscy. "My father just died."

Suddenly they were both stone cold sober, standing there, looking at each other and knowing. Oscy's remark had worked like a bucket full of ice water in their faces. He saw his friend's face and wished above anything that he could have taken back that last remark.

The tears came to Hermie's eyes and poured down his cheeks. He just stood there, biting on his fat lip, his arms at his sides, staring at Oscy. Oscy didn't know what to say. He wished back his words as the tears fell down Hermie's face and crashed to the landing to be soaked up by the carpeting, to join all the other tears.

Hermie spoke, through a baseball lodged somewhere in his larynx. "I can't remember what he looked like, Oscy. I can't remember his face."

Oscy got scared. "Take it easy, Hermie."

"What do I do to remember him . . . look at snapshots? Snapshots are deader than people."

Oscy took Hermie's arm and steered him through the apartment, toward his own bedroom. "It's okay, Hermie. It's all right. It's okay."

"I mean, what the hell is *that?* What the hell is *that,* Oscy?"

"You have to sleep it off, kid."

Oscy helped him to his bed and got him to lie down on it. He slowly began to take off Hermie's shoes, loosened his tie and collar . . . the tears on his face falling to join Hermie's.

"It's going to be fine, Hermie. You'll see, in the

morning, it'll all be okay and . . . you can be anything you like, Hermie. It's okay with me." Oscy found a chair and sat, for the rest of the night, watching Hermie sleep.

37

Hermie saw his mother the next day, and Ruth. They talked little. He suggested Uncle Nat would know what to do with the clothes and things. Whatever he thought best was all right with Hermie. He would straighten out the papers before he went back to school. Ruth breathed a little sigh when he said school, and held her mother a little closer.

Hermie spent the rest of the day going through his father's things. It was an emotionless detail, something that had to be done. He put in one pile the bills that had to be paid. His mother could handle that in a couple of days. The pictures and stuff he put into a shoe box he found in the closet and put that in his own room, under the bed.

He told Ruth what he'd done. She was grateful. She said she could handle the rest.

They put him on the train the next afternoon. There weren't any tears. Just a kid going back to college. As the train pulled out he didn't look out of the window, but concentrated on one paragraph of *Life* magazine until the conductor called his station.

The depot was quiet, dark, deserted, except for a couple of sleepy station personnel. He walked toward the telephone booth, prepared to call the number displayed over the instrument. TAXI. CALL 977.

Just as he reached the booth a car's headlights, suddenly switched on, pierced the night, holding him blind in their glare. Transfixed for a second, the lights went out and he fumbled for his eyesight and a match, to call a cab.

Again the headlights screamed out, taking back his vision and leaving him helpless and confused. Someone was playing an elaborate game. He couldn't cope with it right now.

Out of the light a figure stepped, and coming up very close, to just under his chin, said, "Need a lift, sir? Carry your bag, sir?"

He still couldn't see, but his heart felt lighter. Maybe he could breathe again. "I called the fraternity house and they told me." It was Julie. Thank God it was Julie. "I called your home and your mother told me what train you were on. She was very nice. I'm very sorry, Hermie."

"Thank you."

"I'm glad you're back."

"I don't know. Maybe I flunked out."

"No. I checked your grades. You passed."

"How close was it?"

"You were in the top 90 percent. Congratulations." She moved in closer and put her arms around him, under his coat.

Hermie, still staring into the headlights, said, "You're going to run down your battery."

"Never," she reassured him. She kissed him on the chin, the only part she could reach without his cooperation. Then she moved away and picked up his bag and tossed it into the back of the car. She went around to her side and got in. Hermie climbed in on the other side and closed the door. She started the car and slowly pulled away. "Hear about the fire in Larrabee Hall?" she asked.

Hermie smiled and they drove back toward school.

The Coming of Age

by

Simone de Beauvoir

author of *The Second Sex* and *The Mandarins*

A WARNER PAPERBACK LIBRARY BOOK

72–182 / 864 pages / $2.25

wherever paperbacks are sold

Ⓦ A Warner Communications Company